Shooting Stars

make a wish, seek your truth,
find your destiny

KEVIN S. SPIVEY

SPECIAL BLEND PUBLISHING

I HONESTLY LOVE YOU
Words and Music by PETER ALLEN and JEFF BARRY
Copyright ©1974 (Renewed) WOOLNOUGH MUSIC and IRVING MUSIC, INC.
All Rights for WOOLNOUGH MUSIC
Administered by WARNER-TAMERLANE PUBLISHING CORP.
All Rights Reserved
Used by Permission of ALFRED MUSIC

I HONESTLY LOVE YOU
Words and Music by Jeff Barry and Peter Allen
Copyright ©1974 IRVING MUSIC, INC., JEFF BARRY
INTERNATIONAL, WARNER-TAMERLANE
PUBLISHING CORP. and WOOLNOUGH MUSIC
Copyright Renewed
All Rights for JEFF BARRY INTERNATIONAL Controlled
and Administered by IRVING MUSIC, INC.
Administered by WARNER-TAMERLANE PUBLISHING CORP.
All Rights Reserved Used by Permission
Reprinted by Permission of Hal Leonard LLC

First Edition August 2021

Edited by James Riordan, Courtney Vincento and Caroline Macon Fleischer
Book cover and interior design by Danna Mathias

ISBN 978-1-7355410-2-0 (hardcover)
ISBN 978-1-7355410-1-3 (paperback)
ISBN 978-1-7355410-0-6 (e-book)

Special Blend Publishing
specialblendpublishing@gmail.com

DEDICATION

This book is dedicated to my parents who
showed me the power of words.

To Miss Leveque who taught me how
to use the power of words.

To my wife Faith who used the power of words to inspire me.

To Callie and Company whose comfort spoke volumes.

Foreward

THE PROBLEM WITH MOST STORIES ABOUT LOVE IS that they lose the truth in the romance or lose the romance in the truth. *Shooting Stars* some-how holds onto them both. It is a wondrous story that in some ways feels too special to be true, but in others too real to be special. It is all these things and more and I know the heart of the man who wrote it and it is special indeed.

It's an escape and an adventure, but the situations are so real and the emotions so true that, like even the best of life, it comes sprinkled with pain. It's been said that the greatest hurt is never having tried to climb the mountains of your dreams and dared facing the rapids taking you back down. In our world today, our fears so outweigh our dreams that it is rare to find someone will-ing to take the risk. This is a story about people who did.

By James Riordan

Author of *Break on Through: The Life & Death of Jim Morrison, Stone: A Biography of a Radical Filmmaker, The Coming of the Walrus, The Platinum Rainbow, The Bishop of Rwanda* and others.

Preface

I WOKE UP AT AROUND FIVE A.M. ON CHRISTMAS morning 2016. I wasn't ready to get up yet so I was just lying there when thoughts began racing through my head. These thoughts soon turned into a story. By 6:30 a.m. the story was complete in my head, so I thought I should get up and write down the whole context so that I wouldn't forget it. In the past several years I have been learning to listen to and trust my gut so I thought I should just go ahead with it all and see where it would take me. As Christmas day went on strange things were happening. First, I was watching the CBS Sunday Morning Show and there were three stories on that morning: one was talking about the true meaning of love between two people; the second was the Dali Lama saying our main purpose in life should be to live with joy and seek peace. Then there was a story about the darkest place in the United States to go see shooting stars. The next program that came on was a story about a girl and her father and her name was Emily; the name I had already chosen for one of the characters.

I began to actually write the story two days later. I thought it was coming out very easily but I really didn't know why I was even doing it. It was very visual; it was like I was dictating a movie. By the end of the morning, I had written a couple of chapters before I finally wore out. Over the next couple of weeks, I continued to write enthusiastically but I was discovering that I did my best writing first thing in the morning and I wasn't very good at getting up early so my writing time was limited to the weekends. It was at about the two-week mark that the whole ending of the story came to me so I went ahead and wrote it out of sequence. After that, I went through a very busy period in my life so I wasn't able to write very much and I was starting to worry that I was losing the whole thing. By the time April arrived my brain could no longer hold the story, so I cleared my schedule and just wrote until it all came out. It was around seven p.m. on Sunday, April 23, when I typed: The End. I sat back on the couch, sighed, then turned to the TV. Within a minute a commercial came on that had a shooting star. Before the night was over there was a second different commercial that contained a shooting star.

The main character's name Mackenzie was popping up all over the place, even on a television commercial for a movie that had a shooting star in it. There was another TV movie on the Lifetime channel with its main character named Mackenzie who was writing to tell her story because everyone has a story. Another time I was looking for a profound statement to use at a key moment in the story. I remembered that more than a month before I had gone out for Chinese food with my mother. She gave me her fortune cookie because she doesn't like them. Neither do I, but I do like to read the fortunes. I ate my cookie but put the other one aside. When I was trying to think of something for a profound moment in the story, I remembered the cookie and pulled out the fortune; that fortune turned out to be the statement about how precious time and truth are from the horoscope in the story. Not only was it a profound statement for the story, it was profound for what was going on in my life.

It was May 1st, 2020, when my mother passed away. She was a sharp, 95-year-old matriarch of our family. In the days before her passing, she pulled me aside and told me how sorry she was that she hadn't been able to read my book. It tore me up that I hadn't been able to finish the book in time for her to read it. I was still upset about that as I was by her side in her final moments. Then I felt a peace come over me. She had passed. I looked out the window in sadness. (My mom and dad loved each other more than any other couple I know. My dad passed in 2003 and my mom missed him so much. They loved to dance.) As I continued to gaze out the window, I noticed two bright twinkling stars next to each other. A song started to play in my head-The song was Stardust. That was their favorite song to dance to. I started to smile knowing that they were together again. Yes, time is so precious. Make every moment count.

Chapter 1

HAPPY BIRTHDAY TO ME. IT WAS MARCH 26 AND I WAS experiencing the annual ritual of the birthday celebration. That involved dinner at Red Lobster with my family and eight waitresses (covering all the keys) singing "Happy Birthday." I hated when that happened. That year was particularly distressing because it was the big "five-oh." Everybody was thoroughly enjoying themselves with the endless number of what they believed to be the most hilarious and creative gifts ever given. You know—black balloons, adult diapers, a walking cane, and so forth and so forth. Oh yeah, there was the membership to AARP and then asking the waitress if we can use it for a discount. You get the picture. My wish when I was blowing out the candles was that this would just all be over, but I knew full well that wasn't going to come true; birthday wishes never do. There was the wish for a puppy when I was ten and a new Camaro when I was fourteen. Of course, I knew I couldn't drive until I was sixteen, but I thought that would give the birthday-wish gods some time to work on it. After that I asked for more important things, like passing algebra or going to prom with Olivia Newton-John. I would have even settled for my second choice, Lori Lee, the cutest girl at my school. Nope, I did not even get my third choice, whoever that was. After that I decided that birthday wishes never came true. But wishing on a shooting star, well that's another story.

I was nineteen when a friend of mine asked me to go to Colorado for a "guys' journey" into the wilderness. I had never been out of the state of Illinois and it was a great excuse to get out of work, so I said sure. My friend was several years older than I was but that didn't really seem to matter. We met while we were in a junior bowling league. We got to talking and found out that we both played the guitar. Well, at least I liked to tell people I played the guitar, but that was kind of a stretch. My friend could play and sing, and I could hold my guitar and stand next to him to provide some moral support. We played in a church group and performed at things like weddings or when someone wanted entertainment for free. It was the seventies and John Denver was our hero. He sang about "Rocky Mountain High," so Colorado was the place for us to go.

We decided to reach for the summit of the most hallowed grounds of Rocky Mountain splendor: Aspen, Colorado. This was home to many of the most famous celebrities and of course, John Denver himself. We arrived on a beautiful afternoon in mid-August. We ended up at the town park and met a guy playing his guitar. His name was John, but unfortunately his last name was not Denver. He wasn't any better than we were so we asked if we could join him for a summer afternoon jam session. We played until about dinnertime and then we all decided to take a walk around town and find a place to eat. As we strolled through town, it seemed that every street corner boasted guitar players performing their greatest hits. So, after we found a place to eat (that we could afford), we were all talking about how great it would be to spend our lives playing guitar in this Rocky Mountain paradise.

Then someone came up with a great idea—or at least we thought so at the time. Why didn't we find a street corner and pull out our "getfiddles" and do a show of our own? After all, we had rehearsed for at least an hour, so we should be ready to make our national debut. We had our roadies (us) unload, tune up our instruments, and open the guitar cases to collect our revenue. The management team (again, us) huddled together to discuss our song list and in what order we would perform the six songs we knew. The crowd of one was getting restless, so we stepped onto the stage (literally on the front step of the laundromat). We'd hit the big time! About forty-five minutes later, and more people than we could count on one hand, the crowds finally started to disperse after we completed our sixth encore (we went through our song list twice). We had collected enough cash to buy a case of Coors beer, the champagne of beers west of the Mississippi River.

As we were walking back to our "tour bus," we noticed a crowd—I am sure it was overflow from our performance—had gathered in the center of town. When we looked closer, we saw a pretty girl playing the guitar. For the sake of our art we thought we should give this a closer look. She was quite a good performer. She was good enough to have been our opening act. She captured our attention and kept us there for quite some time. She said she was performing to raise money for her friend who was in the hospital with cancer. The friend's family needed help to cover the bills. Not only was this girl gorgeous — she was also altruistic.

What happened next was something I would never forget; during the next song, my friend took off his cowboy hat and passed it through the crowd. Everybody was putting their contribution into the hat. I couldn't help it; I had to contribute most of our earnings for the night but make sure we still had enough money for the beer. He handed the hat to the girl and she began to cry and simply said, "Thank you." But it wasn't just the words she said. I really could feel her appreciation for this kind act; it was a feeling I would never forget.

By this time, it was starting to get dark and we had no place to stay (that we could afford). So, we did what we came to Colorado to do in the first place: we went camping. We drove several miles out of town and just pulled off to the side of the road. We grabbed our gear and started walking into the night woods. We walked for what felt like an hour but was probably closer to ten minutes. We came to a clearing that was big enough for us to set up camp in and staked our claim. None of us felt like setting up the tents, most likely because there was no light to read the instructions by, so we just built a campfire and cracked open our case of beer. We talked for a while and the campfire was slowly dwindling, but no one seemed eager to go hunting for more wood. That was when our new friend pulled out a cigarette, or so I thought. After further investigation, I realized it definitely was not a cigarette, or at least not like the ones my dad smoked. In keeping with the mission of this trip being the rite of passage into adulthood, I felt it was my duty to continue my education.

The campfire burned itself out and all was quiet, except for the sound of a mountain stream off in the distance. The air was crisp, but not cold, and felt good. I was lying there thinking about how perfect the moment was. I had never seen so many stars up in the sky. As a kid I used to lie on our back porch and look at the stars and dream. I would dream about my future: wife, kids, job, house, and just about everything else, wondering what was ahead for me. And then I saw something. It was a flash that flew across the Colorado sky. It was a shooting star, one like I had never seen before. I was in a bit of awe, then suddenly, I remembered that you're supposed to make a wish when you see a shooting star. So, I made my wish.

But before I could finish, there was another shooting star, and another and another. I thought to myself that this enhanced cigarette was some pretty good stuff. Was this the "Rocky Mountain High" that John Denver sang about? The shooting stars continued to flash across the sky. I started to count them. After five minutes I had counted nineteen. At that point, I decided to just lie back and enjoy the spectacle. I never went to sleep that night. I was making a lot of wishes, but would any of them come true? Then, my thoughts flashed back to the girl singing in the town square earlier that night. I did something I had never done before: I wished for her wish to come true. I made the wish with a deep and sincere desire to see it manifest. This was unlike any of my previous wishes where I was seeking a prize like you get in the bottom of the Cracker Jack box. This felt amazingly good like I had never felt that way about any of my other wishes. Would it come true? I would just have to wait and see, or would I ever know?

As the years passed, many of the wishes I made that night did come true. I got the job I wanted. I was making good money and could afford the car I wanted. It wasn't a Camaro, though; it was a Honda. I met Emily, a wonderful woman with whom I fell in love and got married. I'd never made any wishes about having kids. I wasn't especially sure about that until my wife thought she was pregnant. I wished really hard, and it came true—she wasn't! Everything that I wished for seemed to be happening. But I never knew if that Colorado girl's wish had ever come true. I never stopped thinking about it though.

I continued to make wishes whenever I saw a shooting star. After my experience camping in Colorado, I researched to see if I could find out what was behind all the shooting stars. I learned it was a meteor shower—the Perseid meteor shower, to be exact. It occurs every August. I made a pilgrimage every year to go to a place that was as far away from the city lights as I could find to watch the event. I even tried that special place in Colorado to relive that first time.

I learned why people say you can never repeat experiences like that. First, there was no way I was ever going to find that place somewhere in the mountains near Aspen that had a mountain stream nearby. And second, when you plan something like that, you need to check the calendar to see if there is going to be a full moon at the time. You should do this *before* you plan a whole vacation and spend lots of money. And I guess there was a third thing. I didn't know where the mysterious guy who was our band mate was and where he got his special cigarettes. I tried camping a few times with my wife, but I could never recapture anything close to that experience to share with her. Plus, my wife could not quite get the joy of camping when there were plenty of good (or even bad) hotel rooms available.

After I met Emily, I started bringing her with me to share the amazement of this event. It became something like a scheduled holiday; you know, like Christmas or Black Friday. Every year, you get up at four in the morning the day after Thanksgiving to fight with hundreds of other holiday shoppers to spend thousands of dollars on great deals that you didn't take advantage of when there were even better deals before this shopping day. Emily was never really able to connect the joy of the two. At first, I think she thought it was somewhat of a romantic adventure, but like many things in a marriage it tended to fade after time for her. Eventually it became a "me-time" getaway. Emily was just fine with that. I think she enjoyed having a "her-time" getaway, too.

When she stopped going with me, the experience began to change. Or maybe "evolve" is more accurate. This quiet time was causing me to become more reflective and introspective. My wishes were becoming less about things and more about answers. And each year the questions I had were becoming deeper and deeper—about things like God, religion, relationships, love, joyfulness, and what "peace" really was. The whole experience was becoming very intense and seemed to be rapidly expanding. My time was becoming more meditative, prayer-like. I decided to start journaling these events just so I could remember everything: my questions, thoughts, and desires, and also, the journey I was on.

There was a weekly television show at the time called *Dr. Quinn, Medicine Woman.* One of the main characters was a man named Sully. He was a man of the wilderness, like Jeremiah Johnson, who lived off the land. Much like I did on that trip to Colorado with my friend. Sully was a friend of the Cheyenne in Colorado and spent time learning and understanding their ways. One of the things he learned and practiced was going out into the wilderness alone, without any provisions. On his journey he would stop at a place where he would outline a circle and sit in the middle. This is where he would sit, pray, and meditate for days without any food or water. He would sit there no matter the weather, and would stay until the gods gave him guidance or a vision. It was called a "vision quest." This was now the label I used for my trips to watch the stars. Of course, I would still be taking my traditional beer with me on my quests. At some time, I added popcorn to the tradition. You can't watch a good show without popcorn and beer!

Chapter 2

IT WAS MAY 14, MY MOM'S BIRTHDAY. MY MOTHER WAS in her eighties and had lived alone since my father passed away ten years ago. I tried to go see her at least once a week. She was in good shape and did a wonderful job taking care of herself. My brother and two sisters lived out of the area and were unable to visit very often, which left me to attend to her. Don't get me wrong; I love my mother and she was no burden to me. However, she liked to pull out the "old" card, claiming she needed help when she really didn't. She'd been married to my father for fifty-seven years. They were the happiest couple I'd ever known. They did everything together and I never saw them fight, not once. They took good care of all of us and were the greatest role models anyone could ask for. But she was lonely without him. She would make things up just so she would have a visitor. I knew this and it didn't matter. I would do whatever I could to make her happy.

I always got my mom flowers on her birthday, but this particular morning I was running late and had not gotten them yet. She always worried if I wasn't there at the time I said I would be there. I was panicking because I knew of only one store on the way to Mom's house that carried flowers, but you could never count on the quality of what was available. So, I was driving down the road faster than I should have been and I saw some brightly colored flowers in front of this new shop. It must have just opened because I hadn't remembered seeing it before. The name on the sign simply said "Mack's Store." It didn't say what kind of store it was but they had flowers and that was all I needed to know. I grabbed a bunch and went inside to pay for them. I could not see anybody in the store. My anxiety was growing and time was speeding up. I'd decided I would just leave the money on the counter, when a small dog came running around the corner barking at me like a police attack dog. I didn't know whether to be scared or laugh. Then a woman (I think) came up to me and said, "May I help you?"

I gave her the money for the flowers and she asked me for my name to put into the store's database. I thought to myself, *You must be kidding me; can't you see that I'm in a hurry?* But what came out was, "Brad Norman."

She asked, "Who are the flowers for?"

I replied, "My mother, I see my mother every week . . ."

She exclaimed, "You are a wonderful son to take flowers to your mom every week!"

I'm not sure if it was because of how late I was or because I liked being referred to as a wonderful son who took flowers to his mom every week, but I simply said, "Thank you."

I left the place feeling somewhat confused. It had been a simple transaction. It only took a couple of minutes and very few words were spoken. The clerk was indistinguishable. I couldn't tell her age or anything else about her. She had been wearing dirty, baggy clothes and her hair had been pulled back under a baseball cap. I got back into my car, and when I was on my way, I realized that I still did not know what kind of store it was. I knew right then that I would be going back some time to find out.

The following week I was on my way to visit Mom and I decided I would make another stop at the store. I walked into the shop and the clerk looked different. She was still in work clothes—overalls, I think—but I could see her face better. I thought she was kind of cute, but I still did not have a good look at her. She said, "Are you here to pick up your flowers for your mom?"

"Uhm . . . yeah?" I had no choice but to be the wonderful son who gets his mom flowers every week. So, I handed her the money and she asked me my name again, and I went on my way to see my mom. I learned that people are happier about getting flowers when they aren't expecting them; my mom was really happy.

This continued for weeks. I would go in, get my flowers, she would ask me my name, I would pay her and leave, thinking I still wasn't getting what this was all about. Each week she looked different: her hair, her clothes, sometimes glasses and other times not. She did not have just one style. I could now see that she was young, but I wasn't sure just how young. She looked like she could still be in high school, but how could she be running her own business? I thought she was very attractive, but I was fifty years old and thought she could still be in high school. That put my thoughts back into check. But I did still keep going back.

I decided that I needed to start getting some answers. I just had to figure out what the questions were first. My mom asked me to stop being so wonderful and bringing her flowers every week as she was getting overwhelmed with them. There really wasn't anything else in the store I thought I could use. I had to come up with something. So, I continued to go every week and get the flowers; I gave them to strangers and to my wife on occasion.

I would say I was a happily married man. I met my wife when I was in my late twenties. I was a manager in a retail store and I'd hired her to work in the store. We fell in love and got married a year later. She went to college and got her degree in accounting and got a "real" job after graduation. While she was moving up the ladder and enjoying her newfound success (and money), I was becoming increasingly disenchanted with the whole business world. I was tired of the long hours, bad bosses, and just people in general. I was never driven by money. My joy was in having freedom. I loved being outdoors and having my own schedule. Secretly I wanted to be an author, but my job always left me too tired to write.

My wife, Emily, was a terrific woman. We never fought and we actually enjoyed our debates over our differences. We basically agreed on most things but I liked to embrace the role of devil's advocate, just for entertainment. If she took the side of the Democrats, I took the side of the Republicans (even though I agreed with her). There were those times where this devil ended up in hell. It didn't take too long before she realized what I was doing. Needless to say, Emily is a very smart woman and was pretty good at playing devil's advocate herself.

I would do anything for her and she would do anything for me—and she did. About five years earlier, she let me quit my job so I could try to find my true purpose and achieve happiness. Her job could support us and provide the necessary benefits to a reasonable standard of living, which was good enough for me. She gave up a lot so I could do this and she never complained. We were happy in our middle-class lifestyle, or at least I believed we were happy. We never had any kids, but we had a nice house and car and occasionally got to take a vacation or go on a classy date, or at least on what *I* thought was a classy date. I always told her that if we did that kind of stuff too often it would lose its luster.

But I always felt like she still wanted more—things like a trip overseas, or the ability to start her own business or even to go back to school to be a veterinarian. I wanted more, too, except my "more" was about having the answers to my growing list of questions. Questions like "What is the meaning of life?" and "Is there really a God?" and "If so, what religion is He or She?" Right now, though, my questions were about "What's up with this store?" So, I made it my mission to get some answers.

One week, I told myself that I was not going to buy any flowers. I was going to go there and have a conversation with the clerk. When I got to the store I walked in with a strong, even kind of cocky confidence. I was going to take charge of this conversation. The normal routine began, with the little dog barking up a storm at me and the clerk following right behind. That was when everything changed. This girl was stunning. She was gorgeous, sexy with a smile like I had never seen before. Was this even the same girl from all the weeks before? As much as I tried to justify that it wasn't, I knew that it was her. But how could I have not noticed this...lady? I was beginning to think that turning fifty was causing my mind to malfunction. Everything about me just froze: my thoughts, my body, and most embarrassingly, my words. She asked me twice how I was doing today before I could utter the word "good."

She asked, "Are you getting your mom's flowers today?"

I surprised even myself when I responded, "No, my mom said that she didn't want any more flowers because they were getting to be too much for her to take care of."

"Oh, then what can I get you today?" I hadn't thought about that and my mind was not thinking very clearly at that moment. Then I saw a kitten in a cage with a sign that read "For Adoption." I liked animals but I had never had a pet because of allergies. However, there is a first time for everything.

"I have been looking for a kitten to adopt, so I'll take that one." *What the hell did I just do?!* What would Emily say about me bringing home a kitten without even consulting her? I was certainly going to be in the dog house.

The clerk became excited and took the little kitten out of its cage and handed it to me with a big smile. "It's so great that you are adopting this little boy! Do you need some food for him?"

"Oh, yeah. Sure." The next thing I remember was walking to my car with a kitten, kitten food, kitty litter, a kitty litter box, a kitty carrier, a kitty bed, and a bunch of kitty toys.

Then I remember her saying, "You're doing such a sweet thing, Ben." I was so excited! She got my name wrong but after all these weeks she at least called me something! None of this was exactly what I'd been planning when I went into the store that week, but this attempt at my name was a huge step toward something special. Strangely, I was floating on air when I arrived home.

I got home and saw my wife waiting at the door. I suddenly came back down to earth when Emily said, "So, what have we got here?" I was tense and deeply afraid of what was going to happen next but it wasn't anything near what my wildest imagination expected. She exclaimed, "This is the greatest anniversary present ever! I thought you had forgotten about it!" I had.

The week that followed was wonderful. Emily was so happy that she believed I remembered our anniversary and she really liked having the kitten around. I was actually enjoying having the kitten around, too. And I was happy that my wife was so happy. But I was also happy for another reason; the clerk remembered that I have a name. She didn't remember what it was, but that would come with time. I also became excited when I realized that kittens need food, so I had a new reason to stop by the store every week. All was good. A real win-win.

The first week I went to the store after adopting the kitten, I was full of excitement. The clerk's attempt at my name the week before had me believing that things would continue to progress. I had a plan and I was ready to initiate. I marched into the store ready to fire my charm and hit the target. However, I wasn't expecting the clerk to be at the counter. She was usually in the back and made her entrance behind the escort of the barking guard dog. I was disarmed immediately. She asked, "How is the kitten doing?"

I said, "Great!" and went on to talk for fifteen minutes about every single thing that kitten had done. I just kept going and going until another customer came into the store. I had to just pay her and let her tend to the other customer. She didn't have many customers, so I didn't want to deprive her of any business. What would I do if she ever went out of business? As I was walking out of the store I said, "Have a nice week!"

She called, "You too, Bert!" It still wasn't my name, but it was two weeks in a row that she tried! YES!

Needing kitty food every week made for a nice, and what seemed to be legitimate, reason to go to her store. There really wasn't much else in the store that I could use or even make up a reason to use. It was very eclectic. In addition to the flowers and the kittens (and so many kitten accessories), she had crafts, smelly stuff, horse stuff, cowboy clothes (for a slightly younger clientele than me), farm stuff, and a bunch of other stuff. Every week there always seemed to be new stuff, too.

On one particular trip to the store, I was more relaxed. I did not go in with any plan of attack or hopes of grandeur. I walked in and she was in the front area. She turned around, smiled, and said, "Hi." I returned the greeting. She seemed a bit quiet on this day.

"How is the business going?" I inquired.

"It's slow and hard to compete against the big box stores. People seem to want to save a little bit of money instead of helping local small businesses." This was something I truly agreed with her on and I made sure I let her know I agreed with her. It had to be at least worth a few extra brownie points.

I had worked at a big box store and hated it. I have always been a fan of the little guy—in this case, girl.

I asked her how her going into business had come about. She said she had always loved horses and animals. She started out to be a veterinarian, but that was too expensive and too demanding, so she switched to studying animal nutrition. Once she started feeding her animals healthy food it was costing so much she started a kind of co-op for herself and her animal-loving friends so they could save some money buying food in bulk. It took off from there but so did the costs of running a business. It was getting tougher to survive. I asked her what she really wanted to do with her life; she said anything to do with horses. She said she still had a plan for that but it was going to take some time. I asked how old she was and she told me she was twenty-four.

I said, "Don't be in a big rush. Take some time to enjoy life, it's really all we have." It was unusual for me to say something so profound out loud, especially to someone I really didn't know.

A customer came in so I went and got my kitty food and brought it to the counter. As I was handing her the money, she asked, "So, how old are you, Bob?"

I smiled. "I don't know how old Bob is but Brad is fifty."

She smiled back at me. "Sorry, I don't offer AARP discounts."

I laughed and started to walk away. Then I stopped, turned around, and asked, "By the way, what's your name?"

"Mackenzie, but my friends call me Mack."

"I meant the dog," I joked.

She laughed. "King Bear, but it is spelled B-A-Y-E-R, like the aspirin, because he is such a big headache." She shook her head, smiled, and then walked away.

After all of those weeks we finally had some sort of connection. Yet I didn't float out of the store like I thought I would have after learning so much about her. I was strangely calm. I was still happy and looked forward to whatever the next step was going to be in this . . . well, whatever this was. I kind of laughed at myself because all of this had happened without a plan going into the store this time. I had no preconceived idea of what to expect. I went home and spent a nice evening with Emily, just playing with the kitten.

Over the course of the next week that calm slowly grew into anxiety. I was attempting to come up with our next topic of conversation, making a list of all the next-tier questions I needed answers to. That calm I walked out of the store with the previous week had turned into ecstatic expectation. We were connected now; we could talk about anything. The gates to the relationship nirvana had been opened for us to dance right through. But what were the questions I wanted to ask? I was putting a lot of pressure on myself to come up with the next scene in our story. Not only did I drive myself completely crazy—I felt even worse than I had before the previous visit. That wasn't supposed to happen.

When I got to the store, I was nervous. What was going to happen? I had never been able to come up with that scene to guide me through this next step. So, I just took a deep breath and walked through the door. There was nobody there. I stood there looking around, but Mack wasn't there. Then suddenly, she came through the back door with King Bayer at her heels. "Sorry, I was out back unloading a truck." She was all dirty and sweaty. This wasn't what young and attractive women were supposed to be doing. She seemed busy and, in a hurry, to get back to what she was doing, so I got my kitty food and checked out. Nothing happened. There was no name calling or even a pleasant salutation, coming or going. It was all just a quick and easy business transaction. Had I just dreamed about what had happened last week? There was no evidence that anything had ever happened at all.

The following week was pretty much the same. She was all work and no play. I was starting to wonder if I had said something in our conversation that upset her. Then I thought maybe it freaked her out that I was fifty years old. That had to be it! I was just a creepy old man to her now. I'm sure she had a lot of creepy fifty-year-old men vying for her attention and now I was just another one. All of a sudden, I felt nauseated. I really was an old man now. Where had my life gone? It felt like just yesterday I was a twenty-four-year-old stud chasing after my mare. Now I was destined for my rocking chair. During the week that followed I was depressed. Nothing seemed to matter to me. The only thing that made me feel better was when my kitten occasionally performed one of his cute kitten routines. But even then, I was depressed because he, too, was getting older and losing some of his kitten charm. The thought of eternal youth was quickly becoming a delusion.

As much as my trip to the store did not matter to me anymore, I still had to get my cat his food. I know I could have gone to the grocery store, but his health was important to me so I wanted to continue with the high-grade food. Plus, I still wanted to see Mack. This week when I got to the store Mack was up front. She was dressed very sexy-country-girl. That just made me feel even older and more dejected. She looked at me puzzled, "What's wrong? You look depressed."

I thought that didn't sound like a sexy young girl talking to a creepy old man. I told her that my kitten was getting older and I was going to miss all that kitten energy and entertainment. Now that I think about it, that was probably a metaphor for what really was going on with me.

Smiling, she said, "Well I can take care of that." I started to get really excited until I realized I was still in metaphor mode and she was thinking something totally different. She left the room and came back a minute later holding a little kitten. That was definitely different than what I had been thinking. This kitten was even cuter than the one before; plus, I really was becoming an animal lover. I also had all the stuff for the kitten and I didn't want that to go to waste. So, I was left with no choice but to adopt this kitten, too. It was the best medicine I could think of for dealing with depression. As I was leaving, she said, "I know this will bring back your smile, Brent." Oddly enough, that cheered me up even more.

The next couple of weeks that followed were back to friendly but general conversation. I had resolved that I was simply going to be the nice old guy who stopped by every week to share my wisdom from days of yore with the beautiful young maiden at the beginning of her journey into a life full of promise. King Bayer was back to barking at me and I started to look forward to seeing what adaptation of Brad she would come up with that week. I wanted to believe that she was doing that on purpose, but I never really knew for sure. But above all, I was happy and content.

Things were becoming comfortable between us. Our conversations were general, they were about family and the things that families do—like cousins getting married, the weather, taking the car to the car wash, and, of course, the unlimited number of pet stories. This seemed like it was going to be our niche—a place that we were both comfortable and a place to safely coexist.

I was feeling particularly at ease one week and decided to have some fun with Mack. She had a good sense of humor and I was ready to put this name game to rest. It really was starting to bug me wondering if she knew my name or not. So, I went to the store and grabbed my kitty food and took it to the counter. Mack was already there and she looked up and started to laugh. I was standing there with one of those labels you wear at meet and greets that said, "Hello, my name is Brad." I was also wearing a hat that had "Brad" stitched really big on the front.

Suddenly, she pulled back her laugh as she looked up over my shoulder. I turned around and there stood this masculine, good-looking young farm boy. He looked at me strangely and quipped, "Is your memory so bad that you need to wear stuff so you don't forget who you are?" He said it with a bit of a chuckle and probably meant it to be funny, but it didn't feel that way to me. I was feeling totally embarrassed and humiliated. *Who the hell was this guy anyway?!*

After a moment of awkward silence, Mack said, "Brad, this is my husband, Jessie."

For the first time I knew that Mack certainly did know my name, but it didn't make me feel any better. My heart sank, there was a lump in my throat, and all I wanted to do was run out of the store and never come back. Why did I not know she was married? It shouldn't have mattered, but it did. Why had she not even mentioned she had a husband? I guess when you are floating around between fantasy and reality you choose to omit some things that may interfere with that fantasy—and reality.

With a half-smile and a fake laugh of compliance, I said, "It's nice to meet you, Jessie." I looked over at Mack and she seemed a bit embarrassed, or maybe uncomfortable, but it was something. I did not care what it was; I just wanted to get out of there, and fast. I said that I had to be leaving or the people at the old folks' home would start looking for me. Again, we all chuckled and said our good-byes and I left.

On my way home that day I was lost. I had fooled myself into believing in something that didn't exist. Mack had another life, another world she lived in. I pretended to know that world but truly I knew nothing about her. The story was all imaginary until that day. I really was just the kind old man stopping by every week for a visit and sharing my unsolicited wisdom. Now I felt like I was clueless. I was just a joke.

Chapter 3

EVERYTHING HAD TO CHANGE. I HAD TO GROW UP, have a reality check, and come to my senses. My make-believe world had to end and I needed to return to the real world. I was determined to make that happen. I still had a life to live and things I needed to do with my life, things I wanted to contribute to the world. But I was back at ground zero. This time, the questions I wanted answers to were not about Mack, they were about me. I was swimming through a myriad of feelings: anger, depression, jealousy, hopelessness, frustration, and loneliness, just to name a few. I was in a battle with myself, trying to fight back those feelings with courage, hope, faith, and perseverance. I would win a battle once in a while but I still felt like I was losing the war.

I was lying on the couch one night watching mindless TV when Emily asked me if I was going on my vision quest this year. I was startled. I had forgotten all about it. It was August and the weeks had flown by and my obsession with Mack had totally consumed me. I had lost all track of time. I started to respond by telling her I really wasn't feeling up to it, when I stopped myself and instead said, "Of course I am." I started thinking about how this was exactly what I really needed right now, more than ever. I told Emily that since I'd just turned fifty this would be a good time to go on a more expanded outing. I told her that it would be a good time to take inventory of my life: past, present, and future. I then said I was going to need more time to do all of this, so I was planning for a whole weekend.

I asked her if she was okay with that and she replied, "Of course." I knew she would be fine because it meant more time for her, too. She deserved some time for herself. The past couple of months dealing with me had been quite a challenge with all my moods.

I started to prepare for my quest and my excitement was growing in anticipation for what I believed was going to be a monumental moment in my life. This was not just going to be a battle for me; it was going to be my Armageddon. As I was making my plans, I decided that I was not going to the shop this week. I wouldn't be able to go the following week either because that was the week of my quest. The kids would just have to settle for plain old cat food. I was okay about not going to the shop. My pull toward my vision quest was stronger than anything else. I wasn't even thinking about what was going to happen after I returned home because I really believed that would work out on its own. I had a strong confidence about everything that was happening. I just knew.

I was so excited about going that I packed up my stuff and left a day earlier than planned. On the drive, I was already starting to experience something. It's hard to explain, but questions starting popping into my head. These questions had no specific context, they were just about everything. What is love? What is peace? What is marriage? Is there a God? Why do people believe the things they do? The questions just kept coming. I thought about stopping so I could write them down and not forget them, but I felt I just needed to keep driving and not risk interrupting the flow that was happening. If the questions were important, I trusted that I would remember them.

I arrived at my special place late in the afternoon. There wasn't much to unpack because there really isn't much you need to bring (other than plenty of popcorn and beer). I did bring two books, a pen, and paper along. I thought I might need these this year. I wasn't sure what to bring but I wanted to be prepared for anything. The two books I brought, and I hesitated about bringing, were a Bible and a Bible dictionary.

I grew up in a traditional middle-class Midwestern Catholic home. My parents were not very strict but they did require us kids to go to Catechism every week. Their intentions were good and I wanted to learn, but to my dismay, it seemed the teachers were much more interested in promoting basketball than they were teaching the Word of God. I made an agreement with my parents that I would go to the class for non-Catholic adults who were getting married in the Catholic Church and I wouldn't have to go to Catechism. I think the priest who taught the class wished I had stayed in Sunday school. I always sat in the front of the class questioning everything he was teaching us. I think the others in the class enjoyed having me in the class so they didn't have to talk.

It was during this period of my life that I recognized that I needed answers to everything. I had lots of questions and it seemed that no one was able to answer most of them. I kept asking the questions anyway. For instance, in my class on Catholicism I never got answers that were acceptable to me, so through the years I drifted away from the Catholic faith. I looked to other places and denominations for answers, but all of my attempts ended with the same results. I never stopped believing in God, but so much about religion didn't make sense to me. I gave it one last stretch where I fully engaged in religion. I went to church, Bible studies, took classes, read books, and brought donuts for social time after the service. I even played guitar in the praise group. Still, I had no answers.

Then one day, I finally had enough of religion. I said to God that I knew He was there but asked why He made it so difficult to understand. I was done with it. I told God that I would continue to believe in Him but I was done going to church. I would still pray but He would have to speak to me clearly if He had something to say to me. I would conduct myself in a manner that showed love and care, but I would no longer accept things just because that was what I was told. It was no longer going to be about ritual and the Bible. Hell, even the Church couldn't agree on what the "truth" was. I put all my books away and hadn't looked at them since.

That was ten years ago. I didn't know why I'd decided to bring them with me now, I just did. I didn't even think about the fact that the main feature of these trips happens at night, without lights. How was I supposed to read anything? The daylight hours were intended for sleeping because you were awake all night. It was really silly of me to bring books. As it began to get dark, I prepared my viewing spot—blanket on the ground, bag of popcorn nearby, and of course, the cooler of beer. I had Coors since it was now a legal beer east of the Mississippi River. I was ready for the show to begin. It wasn't long before I saw the first shooting star.

The light show that followed did not disappoint. It was the best one I had seen since my trip to Colorado thirty years earlier, and this was without any additional enhancements, if you know what I mean.

For every star that shot across the sky I had a wish, and following every wish I had a question. Why did I wish for that? What would it change if that wish were granted? Would it matter if the wish was granted? If I got the Camaro that I requested or the girl that I dreamed about would I become a happier person, a better person? Or would I just wish for something else to make the wish I already received even better? Let's say I wished for a million dollars and I got it. Would I spend it all then ask for two million? If I didn't spend it all, why would I wish for it in the first place? Where would it all end? Every time I saw a shooting star, I would make a wish. What would I do next? I would wish for another shooting star, then another and another. All of a sudden, it hit me. As I lay there looking up at the sky watching all of these shooting stars, I realized that every one of those stars were flying through the universe with no end in sight. The universe never ends; it just keeps going. Our wishes were riding the tails of those shooting stars with no final destination. So, what drives us all to keep wishing? Even when we get the things we think will make us happy, our happiness quickly fades and we're back to asking for another wish. Why? What is it that we are all truly looking for? Does it even exist?

This all happened in the first twenty minutes of my private party. It continued throughout the remainder of the weekend. It was a very intense weekend. I felt like my head was exploding! I hadn't even taken my first sip of beer. I just kept asking why. And what did this have to do with anything?

My wife said that I tended to overthink things sometimes. Okay, she said all the time, how could I turn "Twinkle, Twinkle, Little Star" into *War and Peace*? I decided that I was going to change that about myself. I was going to simplify everything. I was not going to leave this place until I had my answers. Now, that was going to be a very daunting task considering everything that was happening to me that weekend, but I felt I could do it— at least that is what I wished for when I saw the next shooting star.

How was I going to accomplish this? For my entire life I always had to have all the answers to everything. It was who I was. It was my driving force. If I couldn't find answers then who would? All I wanted was to be happy. Then I asked myself, what is happiness? I couldn't come up with a definition. So, then I asked myself: if I don't know what happiness is, how would I know when I find it? Where do people go to look for definitions? A dictionary, of course. I just so happened to have a dictionary with me. It was a Bible dictionary, but it was still a dictionary. That kind of freaked me out but that was consistent with everything else that was going on.

I looked for the word "happiness" and it wasn't there. In a Bible dictionary that was three inches thick and 876 pages long and was supposed to define the words to God's instructional manual, I could not find the word "happiness." Yet when you ask people what they want and why they want it, they usually respond with, "It'll make me happy." So, doesn't it all come down to just wishing for happiness? I thought I had found my simple answer. Now what was I going to do with that? I wasn't so sure that I had accomplished what I'd set out to do. I could return home and step back into life, hopefully with some new perspective. There was no manual for how to do this. I would just have to have the courage to trust my intuition and persevere. *That doesn't sound too difficult,* I said to myself. I can tell you this: self-affirmation does not work. I must have repeated that phrase to myself at least a thousand times and I still don't truly believe that trusting your intuition is an easy thing to do. But I do truly believe it is the right thing to do.

As much as I desired the veracious cognizance and sagacity verisimilitude of empyrean quiescence, the intemperance and rectitude of conjunctive stipulation transcendent effulgence caused me to flit to the neighboring impediment. In other words, I despised complicated and convoluted information. I liked things simple. I wanted to spend my energy exercising my new-found wisdom by contributing to worthy efforts instead of trying to navigate through layers of words that I and 99.9 percent of people didn't understand. There seemed to be this misconception that using some big fancy words that no one understands makes you smarter. In my mind, it means the person doesn't understand what they are talking about so they cover it up by using words that I doubt they understand. Language doesn't have to be, and shouldn't be, complicated; it should be simple and understandable.

I attributed my struggles with organized religion to the fact that the complexity of the subject and the extreme diversity of beliefs made it impossible for me to have confidence in any of the information I was studying. How could something as important as the subject of God be so confusing and interpreted in so many different perspectives? So many that the vast majority of major wars throughout history were fought over religion. I could never come to terms with how the core of human existence based on love could be so divided and evil. It always felt like all of the different denominations spent more time trying to prove that their version of God was the one and only version than spent on performing the deeds to demonstrate the whole purpose of God and love.

The topic of God was so frustrating to me. I never doubted my belief in God, but it never felt complete either. Reading and studying the Bible provided more confusion than internal peace in my head. Yet I couldn't discount all of the people who went to church and dutifully studied their Bibles; they were sincere in their relationship with God. I prided myself on being a person who was open-minded and was able to accept different points of view and give others the benefit of the doubt. However, as hard as I tried, I could not convince myself that those people were truly experiencing peace. What were they doing that I wasn't? What was I missing? Was I the one who was wrong for how I believed in God? Could there be only one religion and the true path was to study hard and keep looking until I found that one true religion? Did that even exist? That lack of confidence caused me to stop talking about the subject of God and religion. I didn't feel smart enough to enter into serious debate about which Bible verse was the right verse for whatever topic was being discussed. In any debate that I ever witnessed, there was always one more verse to counteract the verse that was being debated. There never seemed to be an end or final answer. But is that really the point behind God? My take on God was much simpler. How could I contribute something to the world to make a positive difference? I had never really witnessed much discussion about that.

I had spent years trying to reconcile my confusion over the God/religion debate within myself. I had personally given up on church quite some time ago, but I could not let go of the relationship between God, religion, and me. It was a regular item on my vision quest agenda. I would contemplate the subject for a while without resolve before I would just retreat to my default position of not worrying about others and just focusing on my own relationship with God. I had come to my own personal peace about and with God. But I still couldn't let go of my search for understanding the religious side of the coin.

As I had gathered my stuff together for that year's vision quest, my inner voice had instructed me to take my Bible and Bible dictionary. I was becoming quite intrigued. Why did I need to take them? I had never had a feeling about taking anything with me on previous trips. What was going to be different this year? I was getting much better with this "go with the flow" thing so that is what I decided to do. I threw the books into the back seat and trusted there would be a purpose for them.

The subject of religion popped up, just like always, on the evening's agenda and, just like always, I thought about it for a while and then just let it go. Then I moved on to the next item on this year's agenda: popcorn and beer. Things went on like usual. It wasn't until the next day that things went in a different direction and strayed off the normal path. After breakfast was usually when I would go to the park, and sometimes I would read for a little while or write in my journal. I would do this until I couldn't keep my eyes open any longer and then I would drift off into an afternoon nap.

This year I wasn't getting tired, so I decided to look at the two books. I think I might have started to sweat out of the fear of what was going to happen when I opened the Bible. Then I realized it was August and ninety degrees. I am pretty sure that might have been a contributing factor to the perspiration that was running down my face. As I was flipping through the pages, I stopped only when a topic came up that I felt somewhat connected to. I read until that connection faded. I continued to do that for maybe about an hour before I stopped and thought, *Why am I doing this?* So, I put the Bible down and finally drifted off into my regularly planned nap.

When I woke up, I was still thinking about my internal conversation prior to the nap. I started to realize that conversation was coming from my spiritual intuitive side. Now my thoughts started to go down the road of my analytical logical side. Sometime over the years I had learned about the whole brain-dominance thing; you know, right-brain, left-brain. I don't know if there is any science that backs up the theories that some people are programmed to think in a very linear manner (the left-brainers) and others are programmed to think very intuitively (the right-brainers). The theory states that we all have a degree of both, but there is a dominance that leads how we perceive and process information. I recognized that I was primarily a right-brain thinker, but I thought maybe I should look at this from a left-brain perspective. So, I picked up my Bible and Bible dictionary and started over again. This time I wasn't judging out of frustration, or from a point of view where I knew I was right and everyone who lived by a religious doctrine wasn't getting the idea of what God was really about—which was nicer way of saying that they were wrong.

My personal experience of this right-brain, left-brain thing was very confusing for me. I always felt that I was battling between both sides, which many times led me to a stalemate and an inability to actually decide or take a side on an issue. My thinking was that my analysis made me exceptionally qualified to accurately determine the right answer when I finally would take a stance. Yet, if someone made a halfway decent argument I would fall back into the battle for my own settled stance.

It took me years of struggling through this ping-pong game in my head before I was finally able to come to terms with it. Again, the answer was something very simple but very profound for me. It turned out to be a pivotal discovery that changed the way I think, evaluate, and finally come to decisions I could confidently stand by. Instead of it being something I considered a personal weakness or flaw, it became a strength for me, and a pretty strong one at that. Whenever I was faced with a decision, I would take note of the "why" behind my initial perspective. If it was based on my intuition (or gut), which was the more common place, I would then make a conscious effort to critique and validate with logic. I learned to acknowledge the opposite side as a different kind of truth that was just trying to guide me to a complete and comprehensive result. That didn't mean a quick and easy result, but it did mean a result I felt good about. I would let my debate continue for as long as it needed to: patience truly is a virtue. I knew the debate was over when I was at complete peace without any internal doubt about the result. When that happened, there was no longer any simple persuasion to reintroduce confusion. There still could be times that I would return to the process, but that was because new information that I had not been aware of was introduced, which I now felt was relevant. It didn't give me anxiety though. Actually, it gave me an even deeper peace about what the final decision was because I had more information to validate the decision.

This was so instrumental in my life on a couple of different levels. First, having a deep internal peace about what I believed allowed me to live with a confidence. This confidence gave me the strength to trust my intuition and progress in a more efficient and productive manner. On another level, this inner peace provided me with not only a higher tolerance but an acceptance for those who thought differently than I did. I would think that if you were confident in your position on a subject, it would be easy to fight your cause because you just knew you were right and they were wrong. Right?

Well, it didn't work that way for me. That confidence provided me with a patience. Instead of fighting for my beliefs, I was looking to understand the other person's reasoning for what they believed and why they came to a different conclusion than I had. This practice provided me with the opportunity to gather additional information, leading me to re-evaluate my position, which in turn actually strengthened the validation of my position. It also provided me with an insight to what the basis of the other person's position was. This would give me a direction for further debate or discussion to share the reasoning for why I believe what I do and give them some new thinking points that may bring them to their own deeper truth and peace. The truth is that these things should not be about winning or even being right; they should be about becoming wiser and growing as a person.

My focus went from my internal review of lessons I had learned in the past to sitting in the park sweating while holding a Bible and Bible dictionary at my side. I started smiling as I realized I had finally gotten my answer about God, religion, and spirituality. There wasn't a right or wrong way to believe in God or practice faith. We were all created as individuals with different ways of living life, different ways of learning and understanding. Different does not mean wrong, it just means different. If a person finds their fulfillment through religion, doctrine, and going to church, it is not for me to judge, and if I do then I am missing something.

Then, it hit me that I probably would not be where I am with my peace with God if I hadn't gone to church. Religion and the church were a part of my journey, so how could I say that others were wrong for going down that road? My role should not be telling people what they should do but working in partnership with them to a synergistic discovery of internal peace and happiness. Isn't the commonality of most religions to love thy neighbor? Be patient, be kind?

I was still smiling when I thought I'd figured out why I'd brought these two books with me. It wasn't to read or study them, it was to recognize them as tools for those who needed them. They didn't need to be my tools, but it was okay for them to be the tools for whomever wanted to use them. I held the Bible up and held it like a long-lost friend whom I had just forgiven for past injustices. It was the kind of make-up between two people when both recognized that each of them had a role in that past injustice and were now ready to move on and pick up where the relationship had ended. I went to flip my fingers through the pages of the Bible before putting it aside, when the universe—in its undiscerning sense of humor—sent me a message. It was in the form of a piece of paper that fell out of the Bible. It had my handwriting on it but I didn't remember anything about it. I was an avid note writer. I was always writing down some quote that inspired me with the intent of someday putting them all in a book to hopefully inspire others. I would always put that piece of paper in a convenient place where I was sure it would be protected and safe for when the time would come to collect them all. The problem was those notes would remain there, safely tucked away, until some mysterious reason would come for me to find them. Apparently today held one of those mysterious reasons. The note was a quote from the Dalai Lama. It read, *My religion is very simple, my religion is kindness.*

That vision quest had achieved two extraordinary destinations in my journey for truth. The first: I had reconciled my divergent feelings about church, religion, and their followers. The second: I had found my religion and it was simple.

Chapter 4

I RETURNED HOME FROM MY QUEST WITH A NEW EN-
thusiasm toward life. I wasn't sure what was supposed to happen, but I knew something would. Emily was happy to see me
and asked how everything went. I said, "Good, I think."

She commented, "That didn't sound very confident." I de-
flected the conversation to her and asked how her weekend
went. She spent probably an hour enthusiastically telling me all
of the activities she did. She saw friends and went out for dinner and drinks every night and went on shopping excursions
and bought several new outfits. She seemed very happy, even
ecstatic about her quest. She was obviously more excited about
her weekend than she was about mine. But that was okay; I
wasn't sure what to tell her anyway.

The next day was Monday and was time to get back to
normal, for her anyway. I wasn't sure what normal was for me
anymore. I decided I was just going to take things day by day
and see where the path would lead me. I would wake up every morning and take a deep breath and start off on a new

adventure. The first day started off with a bang. I woke up, did some stretches, and went for a walk at the state park. I found a place by the river where I sat and practiced some measured breathing, which led me into a deep and peaceful meditation. After that, I sat at a picnic table and started to write. I filled up about two pages just by journaling about my trip. I had to do that so I wouldn't forget something important. Then, I decided I didn't want to overdo it, so I went back home, saving something for the next day.

The next day, I awoke early again, stretched, and did my focused breathing. I didn't go to the state park to walk because it was supposed to be ninety-eight degrees and I didn't want my mojo to melt away. That night Emily asked if I could run some errands for her over the next few days, and I couldn't say no. The cats had been off the good food for more than a week, so I had to take care of that. By the fourth day, everything was back to the mundane normal that existed prior to my quest. That "normal" included a trip to the shop.

I hadn't thought about Mack at all since my recent journey. At first, I was anxious about going, but I had to grow up; things just had to change and I had to get my life back and move on. I was not going to let this rule my life anymore. This was the chance to launch the new me—the new and improved me. I had to face Mack. If I couldn't do that, how would I face any of my fears? That was not the person I wanted to be, after all. This really wasn't about Mack anymore; it was about me. So, I went.

I arrived at the store and went inside. As usual there weren't any customers and Mack wasn't around. Then King Bayer came running around the corner barking at me just like old times.

Mack was following behind him, right on cue. She saw me and stopped for a second and then said, "Oh, hi. I haven't seen you in a while. Is everything okay?"

"Yes, everything is going great! I took a trip and had a wonderful time. How have you been?"

She seemed a bit stunned, or maybe a better word would be curious.

She replied, "You know, the same old stuff." That comment triggered the thought in me, *Maybe it was the same old for you but not for me!* That actually made me feel like I had progressed. I was feeling like the one in charge of the conversation. Then I went and got the cat food and brought it to the counter and paid for it. As I was leaving, she said, "Thanks Brad. It was good seeing you again!"

My heart started to race a little bit at the excitement of her saying my name, but I quickly gathered my composure as my mind flashed back to my last visit to the shop. I remembered the reality check that had happened and reminded myself that that was not who I was anymore. I needed to stay on my new course, and I did. For the next few weeks, this continued to be the pattern for my visits. They were all very benign and neutral. But each of these visits built confidence and courage in me to become the person I wanted to be. Not just with Mack, but with everyone.

I believe it was early October when I asked her about her husband. Even after our introduction, she never spoke a word of him. I never saw her with a wedding ring, but, looking back, I could attribute that to the type of work she did. I asked her how long she had been married and she replied, "Two years." Next, I asked how they met. "Through friends."

"What does he do for a living?"

"He's a union electrician." I was noticing a pattern here of being very efficient with the words she was using. I thought I had taken up all of the words she wanted to use on the topic, so I decided to move the conversation to a different subject. I asked her if Christmas was a busy time for the store. The bar was pretty low since I never really saw more than two customers in there at one time. She did start talking in a more comfortable tone, but not with a lot of energy. "This is only the second year the store has been open for Christmas and last year not many people knew about us. I am hoping for a better year this year."

I told her that Christmas was not the happy holiday for me that it was for most people; my years working in retail had taken care of that. I asked her if she was a "cheery elf" at Christmas and her reply was something I wasn't sure I understood. She said, "I used to really enjoy Christmas as a kid. I was an only child and we had a small extended family so I got a lot of attention. I was Daddy's special little girl and I knew it. I got all sorts of presents. But as I got older the presents were more related to being daddy's little boy. I started feeling like I was the son he never had. It was kind of embarrassing going to school and telling all my girlfriends about all the cowboy stuff I got. We were not a religious family but my dad made sure we went to midnight services every year. It was always something special. As I grew up things changed. I don't know why, but we just stopped going to church. It's been years now. No one even asks about it."

I didn't quite know how to respond, but I felt a kind of sadness. Never having had children, I can't say for sure, but I think it might have been my buried paternal instinct coming out. I wanted to do something special for her but I didn't know what.

Between that time and Christmas, our visits with each other were brief and uneventful. There were some weeks she was not even there and I think it was her mother who was watching the shop for her. I am not sure what Mack was doing but I didn't want to seem nosy, being an old guy, asking about her young daughter. Parents can tend to look down on things such as that. I had some nice conversations with this lady; she seemed very bright and pleasant. There was a point, though, when I thought I should be careful not to give her the wrong impression; she was more age-appropriate for me.

As I had gotten older the Christmas season had become more of a nuisance than that wonderful time of the year. I am not sure if it was because I didn't have any children or because Santa didn't leave me gifts under the tree anymore; I suppose you would first have to put up a tree to get presents under it. More than likely, it was because I was on his perpetual naughty list. It probably had more to do with how the holidays had become about buying the perfect gift and having the best decorations in the neighborhood. I believed Christmas had become more about money and commercialism than the joy of giving. The new me was sensing a certain sadness or loss of happiness in people, which concerned me. But I also had to admit I was depressed about Mack. Not from the standpoint of the girl of my dreams being a fantasy, but because a girl whom I had come to care deeply about was not happy. The problem was the age-old question: how do we make people happy? Happiness comes in so many different forms, as many forms as there are stars in the sky. How could we make other people happy when we didn't know what made us happy ourselves?

I did know what made my wife happy, so I knew exactly what to get her for Christmas. She was so happy with the first two kittens and Mack had this cute little kitten that needed a home, so I went for the perfect gift again. Why change something that worked? Besides, the last kitten was starting to outgrow the totally cute stage. I was sure this also made Mack happy. She always got so excited when she was able to find a forever home for her animals.

I adopted the kitten two days before Christmas. Mack was in the store that day. I wanted to give her something for Christmas but after thinking more carefully about it and listening to my intuition, I decided that it probably wasn't a good idea. That decision was validated when I asked Mack what she was getting Jessie for Christmas. She said with a bit (a large bit) of sarcasm that she was his gift; what could be better than that? I tried to bite my tongue on that one, but before I knew it, it just came out: "You're on the top of my list!" That didn't have to be taken as a sexual comment, but somehow that's exactly how it came out. I turned a bright red and abruptly said, "Have a merry Christmas!" and started to run out the door.

She started to laugh, "You too, Brad!" Although embarrassing, seeing her laugh and smile before I left made it worth it.

Chapter 5

I DIDN'T SEE MACK AGAIN FOR SEVERAL WEEKS. I WAS sure she was busy with holiday and year-end stuff like inventory and taxes. I didn't want to get in her way. But I was excited about seeing her again. I sincerely hoped that she had found her happiness during that time. My feelings for her had grown into being about her and not so much about me. I was no longer thinking about how to impress her and convince her that I was really the one for her. It was about her happiness; I just wanted her to have joy in her life. I had no idea what it would take for her to accomplish that, but I wished that she could find whatever it was that gave her true contentment.

I went into the store and she was doing some reorganizing. She liked to move things around a lot. She was always adding new and different items to sell. I still wasn't quite sure what kind of store this was, but I found that to be intriguing. It made her laugh when I came into the store and caught her moving things around again. I didn't even have to comment because she knew what I was thinking and I think she liked the fact that it humored me. Quite often I would ask her if she carried some obscure item just to make her laugh. Then there was the day I asked her for something strange and she actually did have it. It seemed like our relationship had really evolved over the nearly nine months I had been coming to the store. I had always been looking for ways to make that happen but I never felt like I ever did. Maybe I was just trying to meet my expectations of what I thought it should have been instead of taking the time to just let things happen.

I didn't know when we went from being an old guy and a sexy young cowgirl to friends, but I was very comfortable around her now and our conversations felt natural. We never really talked about deep things, but it always felt more than casual. It was nice. The age gap didn't appear to matter and there was no sexual tension (which had been most likely coming from me in the first place). She never talked about Jessie or said anything about their relationship and I didn't ask. Nothing had ever been said about the incident when Jessie made fun of me for wearing my name tag and hat. I think we both wanted to forget all about that. But then we all met again.

One day I went into the store and Mack was already behind the counter. I got my cat food and was taking it up to the counter when Jessie came walking out of the back. He said a cordial "hi" and went about what he was doing. He didn't appear to remember me from before; maybe because I didn't have my hat on. But this time, I wasn't feeling like an old man; I felt like a wise soul. I did not get anxious or panic; I was just myself. Mack seemed uncomfortable with him being there. She didn't say much to him or me that day. I just followed her lead and played along. I felt like an observer but I didn't know what I was looking at.

The feelings I experienced that day stayed with me. They became a benchmark of sorts, determining where Mack was with her feelings. I didn't like what I was sensing about her feelings and I kept trying to figure out what I should do about everything. After some contemplation, I reminded myself that most of the progress in our relationship came by not trying but just letting things happen.

In the weeks that followed everything seemed back to normal with our weekly routine. Then there was the week that her cell phone kept ringing while we were talking. She would ignore it until it stopped, then a few seconds later it would ring again. That happened about four or five times. I asked if she needed to get that and she just said it wasn't important. My internal sensory meter went off. It was not good. She seemed upset but she was good at hiding her emotions and I was afraid to trust my intuition. I left the store that day, but I couldn't let go of that feeling. I started believing that my gut was really trying to tell me something and that maybe I should listen. I was getting better about this intuition thing, but it had never been this strong before or felt this important. I didn't know what to do. I wanted to be there for Mack but I also didn't want to overstep my boundaries and risk the progress our relationship had made. I decided I would try not to think about it and just let things happen.

The next day, I went into the store. It was highly unusual for me to go more than once a week let alone the very next day. She was very surprised when she came out from the back and saw me standing there. She seemed exceptionally happy to see me. "What are you doing here today? This isn't your normal day to come in."

I was a bit surprised that she noticed. I didn't have a reason to be there, I just knew I needed to go that day. Even though it was still winter I noticed that she had gotten some fresh flowers in. I grabbed a bundle and said, "I know someone who is feeling down, so I wanted to get them some flowers."

Her response was not what I expected. "Oh, that is very nice of you." She sounded disappointed and kind of depressed, which was the total opposite of when I came in. I paid for the flowers and started walking out the door when she yelled, "Hey! You forgot your flowers!"

I turned around and smiled at her, "No, I didn't," and walked out.

On my way home, I thought, *Wow! Where did that come from?* It was kind of crazy and courageous of me and totally unexpected—for me and her. Was it too much? Was it too provocative? Was I back to being that creepy old man again? Then I realized that I was happy. My sense of Mack at that moment was that she was happy too. My feelings of anxiety and worry were gone. How had this all happened? Where did I go from here? *STOP with the questions and enjoy this moment of happiness!* my head screamed. I then thought, *This must be how it is supposed to happen; so just let things happen.*

As the time approached for my next trip to the store, I was finding it difficult to scale back my anxiety. Strangely enough I wasn't really scared. I actually felt good about myself. I had done something good for someone and there was no need to doubt the impact of the deed. If she took it to mean something different and found it upsetting, I would simply apologize. I didn't think it was going to be an issue though. What was going to happen was going to happen and there wasn't anything I could do about it now. I just had to carry on.

When I got to the shop I stepped out of my car and took a deep breath. I said to myself, "With my luck her husband will be here today." I took a deep breath. "It doesn't matter; I'm prepared for anything."

I was prepared for anything—except what happened next. I stepped into the shop and Mack was at the counter. She looked at me and I froze for the moment. Then she started to cry.

"How did you know?"

"Know what?" I asked.

"Know that's what I needed?"

I didn't know how to respond. She walked up to me and put her arms around me and continued to cry.

All I could think was, *Please don't let anyone come into the store*. I wanted this moment to last forever. No one did come in the store that day while I was there, so we got the chance to talk—for real this time.

I asked her what was wrong and she quietly said, "Everything." I stood there silently, trying to figure out what to say, when she continued. "I never knew how much I wanted to succeed at this store until Jessie told me he wants me to close it. He says he makes enough money to take care of me and that I could be doing something more productive with my time. The store is not worth all the time and money I put into it." She started to sob but quickly pulled back. She continued, "I wanted to prove to my dad that I could do anything. I know the store isn't doing well but I don't like to give up on things. We've only been open for a little over a year and I started out not knowing anything about running a store. But it's more than just that. When we were dating, he said that he didn't want to have kids and he wanted to make the store something we could do together. He wanted a simple life with a house in the country for me and my horses. That's all I ever wanted. He lied to me about everything. I was so stupid to fall for all of that . . ."

I interrupted, "Stop right there! You are not stupid and you do not have to give up on yourself. Love is about listening and caring enough to let a person do what really makes them happy because that will bring them happiness also. Anything else is selfish."

I noticed she was doing less crying and more listening. I continued, "If you want to know what true love is, look at what your dad does for you. His sacrifice is for your happiness and that is all that matters to him. Anyone who takes that away from a person does not truly know what love is. Contributing to someone's happiness is what love is all about. Their happiness becomes your own." As I was speaking these words, they came alive to me. The more I was able to make her happy, the happier I was.

Those words triggered a barrage of memories of the moments in my life that had brought me my greatest happiness. How much happier I felt when I gave someone a gift they really wanted than when I received a gift I'd thought I wanted so much. Giving my mom flowers made me feel so much better than when she gave me a new shirt or the record I wanted. Or when I took Dad to the movies. He took me all the time and it was fun, but not nearly as much fun as when I took him. We would fight over who paid the bill, but now I understood why; we both wanted to make the other happy, and our greatest joy came from making the other one happy. The memories just kept coming. It wasn't a coincidence; it was a pattern that had been proven many times over the years. It was simple yet so powerful.

Why hadn't I seen this before? Did others know this? It was all so obvious to me now. One of my wishes back on my vision quest had come true; I just wanted to be happy. Now I understood what made me happy, so my next wish was to know what made other people happy. If I could make others happy, then I, too, would be a happier person. But more specifically, how could I make Mack happy?

Chapter 6

BY THE TIME I LEFT THE SHOP THAT DAY, MACK SEEMED to be feeling better. She thanked me for being there and apologized for all her weepiness. I told her that her willingness to share her feelings with me actually meant a lot. It showed me that she trusted me, and trust between people was not an easy thing to achieve. We now had something very special between us and I said, "Thank you for that."

With a nice smile on her face she replied, "When two people have a special relationship, they don't have to have a schedule to see each other."

I stood there, puzzled, not knowing what to say. Finally, I went over and gave her a hug and said, "It used to cost a dime to call someone, and now that everyone has cell phones with them it doesn't cost anything. So, every time you see a dime, remember that you can call me anytime for free." I gave her a dime and a piece of paper with my cell number on it.

We spent a moment just smiling at each other then she said, "It's a deal."

As I walked out, I simply said with a smile, "See you soon."

On my way home, I heard my phone buzz. When I looked it was a text from Mack that simply said, *Thank you.*

This started a whole new chapter in our relationship. Our conversations went from once a week to a few texts a week to a daily, free-flowing conversation. It seemed so natural, so easy. We never really talked about our spouses other than a casual passing comment, but even without words she was still saying a lot. My intuition was getting stronger, as was my confidence in trusting it. I think Mack felt that confidence, which made her comfortable sharing her feelings and valuing my wisdom— and it wasn't just about me being a "wise old man." She didn't have to give me specifics about her emotional turmoil because in some strange way I was giving her a calming peace without needing to know the details.

It was now the middle of February, a time that brings fear and horror to the male species, also known as Valentine's Day. This year was going to be quite complicated for me. I didn't think I could get Emily another cat, so I had to come up with something new for her. And what was I supposed to do about Mackenzie? I knew that I probably shouldn't do anything for Mack for Valentine's Day, but my gut told me I needed to, and my gut had gotten pretty wise. She never talked about any plans she had for the holiday but I noticed that she had nothing in her store that even hinted such a day existed. This was significant considering she celebrated anything that even came close to a special event with zest and flair. For example, two weeks earlier, she'd hosted a Groundhog Day event at her store and carried items to sell relating to both winter and spring so she was prepared for whatever Groundhog Joe had to say. She even had a stuffed-animal version of Groundhog Joe—she sold out.

I didn't say anything or ask any questions about my observations; after all, Valentine's Day is about lovers. Even though our relationship had really evolved, this was a line I was afraid to cross. But my gut told me to do it anyway. Valentine's Day landed on a day of the week that I did not normally go to the shop, but nevertheless I went. It was a particularly cold day, so I stopped and got a hot chocolate for her and then I went to the grocery store and picked up a can of whipped cream and a jar of cherries. When I got to the store, she seemed surprised I was there on an untypical day. I told her that I needed some kitty litter (when you have multiple cats you always need some kitty litter), so I picked up the bag and went to the counter and paid for my purchase. Then I set my gift to her on the counter, smiled, and left. When I got to my car, I sent her a text that said, *Thinking of you*, with a heart emoji.

She sent me a text back, *Thank you*, with a heart. Nothing ever was said about this, but my gut was at peace. I knew I had done the right thing. I also came up with a great gift for Emily: a three-month-old golden retriever named (what else?) Valentine Joe.

The next few weeks were back to the normal routine. We were both pretty busy: her getting the store ready for spring and me finally getting motivated to start writing. The writing was coming easily to me for the first time. I must have had a lot to say or maybe it was the years of my life trying to tell me something. I wasn't going to fight it; I was just going to let it flow. I had never experienced this before, so I didn't know what I was supposed to do, but my lessons over the past year had taught me to not force things and to just let things happen. It was now the end of March and my birthday was right around the corner. You already know how I felt about my birthday and I was now another year older from where this story started. I was now going to be fifty-one; that's even worse than fifty. I didn't like a lot of attention for my birthday so I didn't talk about it, but I know for some people it is a big deal. I realized I had no idea when Mackenzie's birthday was. What kind of friend would I be if I missed her birthday? How could I find out without being obvious? If I asked her, she would want to know mine, and at that time it would be an awkward situation. I needed a plan to figure it out. I came up with a great one.

During my next trip to the store I told her that my horoscope that day was crazy! "I don't normally pay attention to that kind of thing but I just happened to check mine." I asked her what her birthday was so I could look at her horoscope.

She started to laugh and asked, "Did you really just ask me my sign?" That wasn't the response I'd been expecting. I really did think my plan was better than that. "I thought that went out in the seventies!" Not what I wanted to hear the week of my birthday. I was back to feeling like a crazy old man again, but this time I deserved it and had to laugh about it myself. I changed the subject and quickly ended my visit. I needed to go back and regroup and come up with another plan to figure out her birthday.

The next time I arrived at the store, I went in and there was nobody around. Not totally unusual, but after about ten minutes I started wandering around looking for her. Even Bayer hadn't come out. I was starting to worry and then began to panic a little bit. I went to the back, where I had never been before, and there was what appeared to be a closed office door. I was getting scared, so I went and opened the door and found her waiting for me. She jumped up and shouted, "HAPPY BIRTHDAY, BERT!" She ran up to me and gave me a kiss. On. The. Lips! I was stunned, shocked, and ecstatic! For the first time in my adult life it really was a happy birthday! Then the reality set in… What just happened? The moment just froze. I can't remember any of the thoughts that raced through my head. She did not seem to be fazed by what just happened; as a matter of fact, she seemed pretty happy and excited about it. She inquired, "What do you think?" seeming to seek approval.

I replied, "WOW, I really wasn't expecting that!" She then took me by the hand over to a small couch with a table in front of it that had one of those big chocolate-chip cookies that said "Happy Birthday" on it.

She asked me if I was surprised and I asked, "How did you know it was my birthday?" Really, I wanted to know how she'd figured out my birthday. She didn't know anyone who knew me and I had never told her. How had she come up with a better plan than I had? I was supposed to be the wise one.

She responded, "I just looked on Facebook." Hm, I had never thought of that.

But then my mind went back to what had just happened: she'd kissed me. She didn't appear to have any second thoughts or regrets about it. On the other hand, my mind was racing. Was I missing something? We sat there sharing the cookie. She smiled the whole time, feeling so proud of what she had done, and there I was, still in a state of shock. All I could think to say was, "Thank you," and I meant that on so many different levels. It wasn't that I was feeling guilty or unfaithful about what had just happened; I just didn't know what I felt. We sat there talking for the rest of the afternoon until I realized I had to get home to go out for my annual birthday dinner at Red Lobster.

As I got up to leave, she gave me a big embracing hug, one that lasted at least five Mississippis. I thought to myself, *How did we go the whole afternoon without being interrupted by any customers?* It must have been the universe working for me. It didn't really matter. What was important was that it happened. That night at Red Lobster all I could think of was how much better my chocolate-chip cookie tasted than my steak and lobster. Happy birthday to me!

Chapter 7

WE BOTH CONTINUED TO BE BUSY THROUGHOUT THE spring—her with the store and me with my novel. Our conversations were fluid and without reservation. It seemed like we could talk about anything, but we never did talk much about our spouses. There were no indications good or bad of what was going on with the other halves of our lives. Nothing more was ever said about my birthday party. I did continue to try to find out her birthday but was unsuccessful. She didn't put it on Facebook; I didn't know you could leave it off. I even asked her straight up when her birthday was and all she said was, "It doesn't matter—age is just a number." That's what I always said, but I thought that was just me trying to minimize my continuing rising age. The way our relationship was going, the age thing really didn't seem to matter; it seemed irrelevant. That was fine with me. I was old enough to be her father but I felt young enough to be well . . . I guess anything. Age was never a topic of our conversations.

As spring went on things just went smoothly without any out-of-the-ordinary situations. Sometimes I would stop by and if she was really busy, I would jump right in to help out. It didn't even matter when a customer came into the store. We would just keep going with whatever we were doing, not like in the old days when our day would end whenever a customer entered the store. I even got to the point where I was running the register. On occasion, she would even let me mind the store while she ran an errand. It all seemed very normal to both of us. Some days I would bring lunch and we would sit at a picnic table outside and just talk, her stories and mine. As summer took over, I would bring ice cream from Dairy Queen. She really liked Peanut Buster Parfaits.

It no longer felt like I was a customer but more of a business partner. I started using some of my retail experience to help refine some (most) of her business practices. I was doing some covert marketing along with some Retail 101 practices. It had to be covert because she was very possessive about her store, and it was *her* store. Business was picking up and she did notice. She and I never talked about it, but I knew she knew what I was doing. That was okay because I wasn't telling her what to do. It didn't matter to me whether or not she gave me any credit; all that mattered was her happiness. She actually started turning some things over to me that she didn't like to do or know how to do. She even started asking me to do some of the things I was already doing so it felt like they were her ideas. Whatever we were doing, it was working; we made a good team.

My new role was making my other life a bit complicated. Emily knew I was spending "some" time with Mackenzie, but I kept the actual amount of time vague. My approach to writing changed. I could not focus on creating stories. Whenever I tried, my mind would jump back to the time I was spending with Mack. There were a lot of things going through my mind, but I wasn't sure what to do with it all. I was sure there had to be something in there for me to tell. I couldn't keep up with all that was happening in my head so I started to write it down.

My writing fiction had turned into journaling my story. Telling the truth about what was happening was so much more interesting than anything I could create. It was also making me think about life, real life, and all that meant. I was still contemplating all the questions I had at my last vision quest and journaling was helping me to sort through them. It was pushing me to find the answers through observing real life and paying attention to others. I started noticing that things were making sense. I was experiencing peace. It was hard to explain, but I felt that the journaling I was doing was writing the story I needed to tell. I stopped trying to justify everything I was doing and just go. After all, that was what was working for me. I didn't know why I kept forgetting that and tried doing things the hard way.

Emily always knew I was different and understood that my ways were unconventional. I didn't know why, but she did. I loved her for that because her trust and support were what kept me going and kept life from taking control over me. I knew it was very difficult for her because I am sure she felt like she was on the outside. I knew I was being distant with her and I was sure that had to hurt. It wasn't that I was trying to keep any se-crets or go behind her back with anything. I just did not know how to explain what was happening to me. I couldn't explain any of this to Mack either.

One question that was really taking up a lot of territory in my mind was about what had happened with Mackenzie on my birthday. We never talked about it, but I couldn't forget. I could trace so much of the change in our relationship back to that day. There had been no further physical or sexual innu-endos since that day but she had been so much happier and comfortable with me since then. Was it innocent and I was just making up some story to boost my fifty-one-year-old male ego? My gut told me differently.

Summer had come and the days had turned hot. With the heat came tank tops and shorts. As much as I tried to be a re-spectable gentleman and not objectify women, I was still a man and Mack was still a woman—an incredibly beautiful and sexy woman. Combine all that with my birthday present and I had confusion. I had always been attracted to Mack but I knew that nothing would ever happen between us in that way. Still, she *did* kiss me on the lips. She and I never got into conversations about our sex lives. We did have conversations about past re-lationships, dating, and the rules of the world when it came to these topics. We did have the same opinions on love, sex, and societal norms, but it was always discussed from a third-person perspective. Even this perspective contained many clues to our own realities. I never talked about my beliefs on this topic with anyone other than Emily because I did not believe anyone else would share my beliefs and they would think I was a nut. I was at peace with my beliefs because Emily and I had come to the same belief after more than twenty-five years of marriage and deep, intimate, and honest conversations about the topic. Now I was thinking Mack and I were on the edge of jumping off the cliff and I wasn't sure if there would be a safety net to catch me. Having this conversation with Mack could change everything about our relationship and I wasn't willing to risk that.

At least for the moment I wasn't. The possible catastrophic collapse of the distance we had come in our relationship was far scarier than whatever could come from having this conversation. So, for now, I decided to stay on that cliff, but I wouldn't go too far away just in case I would change my mind and take the jump. But as I was getting to know myself better through all my journaling, I knew that the day would come when I would make that leap. I had to keep telling myself to remember to trust my gut and that everything would be okay. My gut would tell me the where, when, and how. I would just have to remember to not let my hope and expectation get in the way. Our worldly desires and egos can really distort the truth, leading us down the road of misguided direction with dangerous consequences. That is when the truth becomes a lie. That would destroy the whole purpose of my journey to find my truth.

Chapter 8

WE WERE IN THE MIDST OF SUMMER. TRAFFIC AT THE store continued to increase as more people discovered they could find things with her eclectic inventory that they couldn't find anywhere else. The Fourth of July had just passed and everybody was going full throttle with their summer activities: landscaping, little league games, vacations, washing cars, and going on picnics. It was all different for me. I was helping out a lot and it was like I was a high school kid stocking shelves. I didn't mind though. I wasn't upset or jealous of everyone else's summer fun. I was being amazed and entertained with her success in spite of breaking all the rules of retail. I was paying attention as a passive observer. I'm sure I was invisible to them, just a retired old man working to survive.

Up until then my whole summer had been working at the shop or sitting on my front porch writing about my observations of the day. As I watched people, I would look at them very carefully—their faces and eyes. I would begin to create a story about them. At an early age I saw a news reporter who did a weekly series called *On the Road* where he traveled the country meeting people and reporting their stories. He said everyone had a story. That sentiment always stayed with me. Now I wanted to know everyone's story. I wanted to know what their job was and why they had chosen that field. What was their family like and were they married, divorced, or something else? What were their hopes and dreams? What were their favorite experiences and memories? But all of their stories were being masked by their immediate need to buy flowers to plant in their garden or pick up a bag of dog food or kitty litter because it was on sale. They didn't care about my story and they didn't have time to tell someone (especially someone they didn't even know) anything about their own. So, I would make up my own stories about them. I felt an eerie sense of their pain, fears, hopes, and destinies. Even in my make-believe world, no one had the same story; each had their own. My increased journaling of my story had made me much more aware of how many chapters and experiences I had had that I had just forgotten about. However, in retrospect, they still had an impact on my life. Was everybody's life and story like that? Then, my mind went back to that news reporter and his series; he would throw a dart at a map to determine his next destination and when he arrived, he would pull out a phone book and blindly pick a name. This would be his next subject. The randomness was what made the stories so interesting. It was anybody anywhere. I was just another someone who lived someplace; so was everyone else who passed by me, and we all had our stories to tell.

Then one day at the store, things were quite busy. Mack was carrying stuff out to people's cars and I was running the register with half my brain while the other half was creating all of these people's stories. At a brief pause, Mack looked at me and asked, "What are you thinking about?"

It caught me off guard. I didn't know what to say, so I said, "Life."

She quickly responded, "That is better than the alternative."

"Are you sure?"

Then she commented, "I would like to go there sometime."

I am not sure exactly what that meant but it felt like an introduction to a conversation we were going to have at some time. I would just have to wait and trust what this was going to be about and when the conversation would start.

Spending all this time at the shop and writing did not leave me much time with Emily. She never said anything to me about it though. Occasionally, she would ask how my day was and I would simply say it had been alright. Sometimes she would give a cursory hug with a slight smile. I always knew that she was concerned about me, but she felt emotionally distant. It wasn't that I was trying to be that way. It was just that I was so deeply introspective that my whole being was in another universe. But she was still my rock-solid foundation that kept me going. Without her I would have never had the opportunity to find my peace. I hoped she knew that, but I never could find the words to tell her. That would be as far as it would go.

My conversations with Mack at the shop were increasingly fluid and easy. I didn't know if I was talking so much or if she was just listening a lot. I started talking about my past, my life experiences, and how they made me who I am. I had become a storyteller sharing funny, embarrassing, and sometimes very intimate details of my life. We only had short periods of time to spend in conversation each day, but it became a regular part of our day. It didn't matter, though; we always seemed to pick up right where we had left off when we were interrupted. She began asking me questions and was becoming very inquisitive about my life. This was not typical of Mack; she kept her emotions close to her heart. She also was not very good at sharing her own stories. It was very seldom she would bring up any details of her past, and even then, she would only talk about herself if I specifically asked her. She would always say she didn't have any interesting stories to share and then deflect the conversation back to me. I kept talking because I sincerely felt she was listening and trying to understand me. These talks, along with my journaling, stimulated my thoughts, and my writing was becoming almost obsessive. That might have been why Emily was being so supportive; I was actually creating something even though she never asked what it was that kept me going.

It was a Monday when I drove up to Mack's shop and noticed that her pickup truck wasn't there. I was surprised because she hadn't mentioned anything about taking the day off. I went in and her mother was running the register. I didn't know what to do because I was sure Mack had not said anything about me, or me being there every day helping her out. So, I had to improvise my reason for being there. I picked up a bag of kitty litter; as I have said before, you can never have too much kitty litter with three cats. I went to pay for it and asked where Mack was, like any concerned customer would. Her mom was always very nice and made me feel welcome. She said that Mackenzie had fallen off her horse and messed up her leg. It wasn't broken but she would have to stay off it for a couple of weeks.

Why didn't she tell me?! Why didn't she text me?! What was I going to do?! I had no job to go to and no one to talk to. I felt lost. I wanted to go see her but I knew that would not be good. I wasn't sure what her family knew about our relationship and just how much time we actually spent together.

Mack's mom had her own job working at the local park district. Its busiest season was the summer, of course. This was going to create a difficult situation for both Mack and her mom. Her mom couldn't take time off to care for the store and was already worried that her boss would not be too happy with her taking today off even though it was an emergency.

After I left the shop, I drove down the street and immediately sent Mack a text to see if she was alright. She quickly responded saying she was okay and how sorry she was for not being there today. She apologized for not giving me a heads-up. The pain killers the doctor gave her really knocked her out. She said she would be out of the store for a few days, but she would need some help when she returned. She actually offered to pay me to come in and help her out.

I asked, *How much?*

She responded *LMAO*. I had no idea what that meant, but I was too embarrassed to ask. I found out later that was young speak for "laughing my ass off!" I finished the conversation by saying I would be willing to do it as long as it came with a retirement plan. She sent me a text back: *LOL*. I knew what that meant.

So, Mack told her mom that I would be helping her out at the store. Her mom was curious as to why Mack would ask me to do something like that, but after Mack talked with her mom, she thought it would be okay. Mack and her mom got along fine but they did not have that strong mother-daughter bond.

Her dad was a different story. Mack was his "little cowgirl." She was his tough and strong boy he never had, all wrapped up in a cute and sweet package. She was quite spoiled and she knew it, and so did he. But he didn't care. She was everything to him as he was to her. He was not going to let anything happen to his little girl. He did not know anything about me. Her mom knew me from being at the store at times when I came in to "shop." When the idea of me helping Mack out in the store reached her dad, he was very clear that he did not like the idea. Why would this fifty-one-year-old man want to work in her store? The only perception he could come up with was that I was out for something—something like his twenty-five-year-old married daughter. He was a man, so he had a pretty good idea of what men were like.

Mack talked about her dad a lot. He was her hero. As I listened to her talk, at times I would think that the problem with Jessie was that he could not live up to the standard that had been set by her dad. I didn't know if any man ever could. Her dad's solution to this problem was to cancel his fishing trip and use his vacation to help Mack out at the store. When Mack sent a text of his plan, she was very straightforward and did not express any sort of opinion on the matter. This was consistent with the fact that I had never heard her say anything that was even close to challenging her dad's wisdom.

I wasn't sure what I was supposed to do with this whole scenario. This would be the longest stretch of time in over a year that I wouldn't see Mack. I started to fear that this was the beginning of the end of our relationship. We had come so far and things were truly wonderful between us. Her folks now knew all about me. I wasn't sure what her husband knew. I was the creepy old man again, but at least this time it wasn't Mack's impression. But there was nothing I could have done about this. It was what it was and that really sucked. For the next couple of days, we continued to text but it was just not the same. All of the conversations centered on how her leg was doing and what was I spending all my time doing. I didn't know what to say, so I just started to make things up. Things like mowing the lawn, cleaning out the garage, and cooking out on the grill. None of it was true, but it was what everybody did in the summer, wasn't it?

Then on Saturday evening I received a text from her that said, *You're hired and you start on Monday. Don't be late!* I had no idea where that had come from, but who was I to argue with her? I didn't care about why things had changed. I was jumping for joy that we were going to be back together again. I responded, *Yes, ma'am.* I didn't hear from her for the rest of the weekend, but that wasn't unusual. That was family time and it was difficult to have meaningful conversations via text anyway. And besides, it just built up the anticipation of seeing her again. I was so excited I actually went out and mowed the lawn.

Chapter 9

ON MONDAY MORNING, I FELT LIKE A TEENAGER AGAIN going to my first day of work on my first job. It was great! I got to the shop before she did. When she arrived, she opened the door to her pickup truck and I said, "It's good to see you."

She proclaimed in a firm boss-like voice, "Get over here and help me to my throne! And if you ever call me *ma'am* again, I will personally feed you to the lions!"

"Oh no! Not another kitty cat!" We both had a good laugh. Being with her again was even better than I remembered. It felt like our relationship had taken another step forward. I offered her my hand as she stepped out of her pickup truck and she grabbed it. I put my arm around her so she could lean on me as we walked into the shop, but to my surprise, she took a leap into my arms so I had to catch her and then carry her into the shop. When we got to her chair she paused for a moment as if she didn't want to let go. Maybe it was just me, because I knew I didn't want to let go of her. I was waiting to hear what her first words that weren't a command were going to be. As I was waiting for that conversation to start, a customer came in, then another one. I don't think she'd ever had so many customers at the same time, and of course it had to be today! The whole day was like that. We didn't even get a chance for lunch. It really felt like the universe was against us . . . until the end of the day. Shortly before closing, she asked if I had any plans for dinner. Jessie was going fishing and she was on her own. I said, "How about pizza?" We ordered and had it delivered. I had a strong sense that she wanted to talk and my gut was right.

For the first time in our entire relationship she did most of the talking, and she had a lot to say. Like I have said before, Mack did not like to open up and share her personal thoughts and feelings. Today was different. She started off by saying that she had really missed me. She continued by telling me that being sidelined by her injury had forced her to slow down and relax. She said that slowing down was not very relaxing! This was entirely not who Mack was. She said at first she thought she was going to explode! Then she said she started to think about me and how I was always so patient with things like people, animals, and life overall. I had impressed her with my calm and easygoing demeanor and my sage wisdom. My ability to observe people and be sensitive to their needs without any regard for my own was something she was beginning to appreciate and desire herself. She was paying attention to others' interactions with the world and seeing that everyone was so busy trying to be the best—the best parent, the best lover, have the best car and the best house. Why did it really matter? She said that she noticed that I was never trying to be better than anyone and that I really didn't care about things or money, yet I seemed so happy and at peace.

That had always been the destination point of my life's journey, my wish from a shooting star. Had I actually reached my destination? If so, why did I not know that I had? The longer I thought about it, the more I started to think that just maybe I had arrived. I was happy and peaceful sitting with her having an intimate conversation. I needed nothing; I only wanted to feel happiness and joy for others. I was only unhappy when I was around unhappy people. Even then I was energized by trying to help others understand what it felt like to be happy. This was the first time anyone had ever said that to me, and it came from her. She had been paying attention to me and not just hearing but also listening. But now I needed to listen to her.

She went on to talk about her relationship with other people. We had already had many conversations about her mom and dad but this was the first time she said anything about her husband. It wasn't much, but it was still something. She told me what attracted her to Jessie—she never used the word "love" when talking about him—was that he had seemed like the type of guy who would make a good husband. He had a good and stable job, he liked working with his hands and could fix anything. He seemed to get along with everybody, especially her dad. And he was a cute farm boy (she said this with a bit of a giggle). She came to find out that marriage was much more than all of that—and that marriage was something hard to define. Jessie was a "good" guy. He wanted to do the right thing and he believed that he loved her. Mack thought she believed that too, until she started to look deeper. What appeared to be love on the outside did not feel like love on the inside.

She said that neither of them was any good at talking about their thoughts and intimate feelings. She thought that understanding each other was just something that came naturally over time. That was, until she started to get to know me. I was the first person she'd ever really known who would talk like that. She said it scared her at first but then she began to see the kind of difference it could make in a relationship. She said she'd started opening up to her parents.

First, it was her mom. Even though she was closer to her dad, she felt that her mom was more likely to open up to her. She said her mom and she actually started becoming close and sharing things that made her feel more like a best friend rather than a mother; it was changing their whole relationship. Mack discovered that her mom had gone through many of the same issues when she first married her dad. Mack found that to be shocking but continued to delve deeper. Her mom was encouraging her not to give up and explaining to her that men were not very good about sharing their feelings. She said it made them feel vulnerable and weak.

Mack told me that was when she began to talk to her mother about me. I started to get a little nervous about where this was all going. After all, her mom was from my generation. Her mom pointed out to Mack that me being open with my thoughts was not the norm and it was a special trait for men. The more common scenario was the type of relationship her mom had with her dad. Her mom told her that she'd had to learn to read and try to understand what her dad was thinking and feeling because she knew he wasn't going to volunteer anything. She knew she loved him because she did feel something special, but it took her time to figure how to make their relationship work. Once she figured it out, it became a sixth sense.

Mack said throughout these talks she realized that was exactly how she and her father were. They never needed to have deep conversations because they just knew what they felt about each other. It came naturally. Mack had concluded that that was how love was supposed to be, and that was the expectation she'd had going into the marriage with Jessie. Although she had not been married very long, she already knew that wasn't going to be the case. She took the blame for that because Jessie seemed so sure about his love for her and she just went along with it.

Mack realized that her mom and she were really very much alike. The difference was that her mom had never had an outlet for the way she was feeling—at least not until now. The conversations Mack was having with her mom were changing her life in a big way and for the better. Mack said that when she started recognizing the traits that she and her mother had in common, she also started having a better understanding of her dad. These same traits, however, were also helping her to understand her feelings about Jessie, but with a different result. Mack's mom's realization from their conversations helped her to understand something too: I was something good for Mack.

Then Mack stated that things were more challenging with her dad. When he found out about me helping out at the store, he was able to show quite a bit of emotion, but not the warm and fuzzy kind. He had absolutely no doubt what my intentions were and he would not have any part of it. This was not going to happen. End. Of. Story. Mack was so upset, she ran through her pain out of the house into the dark night.

Mack said she was totally confused. Her dad had never spoken to her like that and she felt like he didn't trust her. That was devastating to her. As she and her mother were becoming close, she and her father were falling apart.

Then, a strange thing happened. She wanted to talk to her dad—I mean really talk to him. This terrified her but she thought about how talking to her mom had created a whole new dynamic between them. She decided she was going to have a "real" conversation with her father.

Mack had not spoken with her dad since he exploded at her regarding me helping out at the shop. Every morning she would go to her parents' house to take care of her horses. Since her accident her parents had stepped in to take over her tasks. On this occasion, she had spent the night outside under the stars. When her father came out to take care of the horses that morning, he stopped, and then there was an awkward silence between them.

Then Mack told her dad, "We need to talk."

Her father responded that he was done talking and he was going to cancel his fishing trip to use the time to work at the store. He told her that she didn't need anyone else to help her.

Then, in a totally out-of-character voice of authority, Mack stated, "Maybe you are done talking but I haven't even started! I am an adult woman and totally capable of making my own decisions. I am strong and I can handle myself if anyone tries to take advantage of me. You taught me that. This is *my* store, *my* accident, *my* problem, and it will be *my* solution!"

I sat there stunned with every word that Mack was saying. I felt like I should say something but I could not come up with any words before Mack continued.

"All my life you have been there for me and taken care of me. Now it's time for me to take care of me. You have not even given me a chance to discuss this situation with you and yet you have decided for me what I am supposed to do. No, it's not going to work that way anymore. We can work things out together, but it is my life and my decision."

She stopped for a moment, then she said she noticed tears in her dad's eyes. She had never seen him cry before. Her heart sank and she began to choke up. She knew this is where she needed to stay strong and speak the truth. She went on to explain our relationship to him. "I know how this all looks but there is much more to the story and you need to hear it. This has been going on over a year without Brad trying anything. He has been kind and supportive of me and I have learned so much from him."

I was pretty shocked at all the good things she was saying about me. I never really knew she felt that strongly about me. I still wasn't even sure if she remembered my name.

She told her dad, "You really need to trust me; I'm a big girl now." She said that when she left, she wasn't sure where things stood between her and her father.

As a tear came to Mack's eyes, she went on to say that later that afternoon her dad stopped by her house and asked if she wanted to go on a drive with him. It would be just Mack and him. They hadn't done anything like that since she was a little girl. He drove to a local park that had a pond full of ducks swimming around. It was a place he used to take her as a child. He'd brought a bag of bread crumbs to feed the ducks just as he had years ago.

But that was when things changed. In the past they would just sit there and feed the ducks and he would give them names and create stories about each of them. Mack said she immediately thought of how I created stories of the people I watch. She said for some reason it opened her eyes to the idea that there was a part of her dad that had a story he wanted to tell. Breaking with the tradition of the past, he told her, "I love you so much and I am so proud of you. It is very difficult for me to tell others how I feel about them. You have taught me something, and that something is how important it is to let people know how you feel. You don't know how many opportunities you have to express that and the longer you wait the fewer chances you have.

"Your mother has made it easy to love her. She understands me and lets me be myself and accepts me for who I am. That makes her a better person than me—just as you have been for saying the truth. It is time for me to stop being selfish and be a stronger person instead of making others work so hard to prove their love for me. It is time for me to share my love for them."

Mack hadn't seen that coming. She said she had wanted to say something, but no words came to mind. Finally, she just asked her dad, "So, when will you be back from your fishing trip?"

There was a silent pause, but he had a slight grin on his face. He quietly said, "Next Sunday."

"Thank you."

Between her tears she told me. "I never really got our relationship over this past year, but felt like there must be some reason for it. Now I know—you are my guardian angel."

Now *I* wanted to say something, but no words came to mind. I wanted to cry but couldn't. Finally, I said, "Thank you."

Chapter 10

———

THE DAYS THAT FOLLOWED STAYED THE COURSE. WE continued to have in-depth conversations about almost everything. I think she felt she had said everything about Jessie that she had to say, because she did not say anything more. She did continue to talk about her mom and dad. She was really excited by how her relationship with them was progressing. She said it was turning her whole family around—a whole different dynamic. She told me that her mom and dad were like two teenagers in love—all "giddy" and everything. And then she smiled and giggled. I didn't say this out loud but I thought about how different she was acting: smiling and laughing a lot. As good-natured as she was, she was not like that very often. She was talking about experiences she'd had growing up, but it was from an entirely different perspective than how she'd previously talked about her past. It was like she saw everything with a new understanding. She was recognizing how her past had shaped who she was now and how reliving those moments through a new set of glasses was creating a whole new person.

She was full of vigor, a kind of "born again" experience, but not in the religious sense.

Mack and I talked about religion sometimes, but it was always very benign. She told me that her family was Catholic but really was not involved with the Church. They went to Mass on Christmas and Easter when she was young but even that didn't happen anymore. She said she never really thought much about it. She said she believed in God but could not really explain what that even meant. She struggled with that at times because how could any God let so many bad things happen to good and innocent people? She said she also struggled with the fact that there were so many rules to being a Christian. When she asked me what I believed I would give her pretty much the same answer every time and leave out my whole dissertation on the subject. I knew she wasn't ready (or even interested) in my detailed explanation. I had started to feel that that topic of conversation would resurface soon because I think Mack was seeking some higher truth to what was going on in her life. I was right.

One day, out of the blue Mack came to me and asked if I ever went to church anymore. I told her that I went for family events such as weddings, baptisms, and that sort of stuff. She asked me if I ever thought of going back to practicing my religion. I told her no because I had gotten to a "different place" in my understanding and relationship with God. I had separated my beliefs from religious doctrine and I had come to a place where I found the peace for which I had always been searching. My experience with religion only confused me and put me in a perpetual state of internal battle for what was truth. I told her that learning to listen to my intuition after clearing myself through meditation and contemplation had guided me with clarity and peace when I trusted it. There were still battles to fight but I knew where to find truth and if I stayed strong in my search, I knew the right answers would come.

"So, you don't believe in the Church?" she asked.

I said that it was not for me but that I didn't believe that it was a bad thing. I told her that I'd struggled with it for a long time and even condemned it, but after going through my process I learned that the Church was a big part of my journey to finding my peace now. Who was I to say that it was not another person's journey? My journey continued because I kept questioning until I found the peace for which I was searching. I now believed that a person's journey would only take them to their destination that gave them peace, whatever that may be. I felt many people stopped short of their destination because they gave up or tried to figure things out that they never would through religious doctrine. Or they just ended up accepting the doctrine because they felt they were not capable or smart enough to understand.

"What prompted you to ask me about this today?"

She sat there silently for a couple of moments, "My family went to church together yesterday."

"What motivated that?"

"Because my father wanted to." She went back into a silent, emotionless pause before saying, "I felt it was a big move for him, an effort at him finding direction."

"I feel a 'but' coming on."

She half smiled and said, "But I didn't feel any comfort by being there."

I told her that was okay. She would find comfort from asking her spirit guide directions for her journey, and then not stop until she found her peace. "Don't judge the Church or others; only judge yourself on your own peace."

This conversation was at a level that Mack and I had never reached before. We delved into a deeper place, a very guarded and personal place for her. She wasn't afraid, though; she kept going. "How did you know when you got there?"

"When you told me."

She had a perplexed look on her face that told me she had no idea what I was talking about. So, I continued. "You told me how patient and at peace I was with the world around me, how I wasn't consumed with money or being better than everyone else."

She exclaimed, "That was just last week!"

"Yes, it was." I went on to tell her that you don't always know when you're at peace until someone else recognizes it for you. But once you know what peace looks and feels like, you know what to aim for. A customer came in and the conversation ended. It was a while before the topic presented itself again.

Our general conversations continued to be more in depth about a wide variety of topics. It wasn't until the end of the day on Friday that she returned to this subject. She waited until she put the closed sign on the door and then said, "I don't know what I am supposed to do about church if my dad wants to go again." I asked her what the problem was and she said she wanted to go for her dad but she didn't want to pretend to be interested in religion.

I said, "Then go for your dad, which is the truth. You do not need to justify anything else to anybody."

"Duh! I wish I was smart like you."

It was kind of a light moment but our eyes locked on to each other's with a sort of cosmic connection that hadn't happened before.

On Sunday evening I received a text from Mack asking if I could get to the store early the next day. I asked if something was wrong and she said no, she just wanted to talk. For some reason this made me feel really good, kind of like when she remembered my name.

We both got to the store an hour early and she was so excited. She started by telling me that she went to church with her family again and had a totally different experience. No, she had not become "born again," but she was totally comfortable being there with her non-religious position just like I had explained to her about my experiences. She also felt a deep connection just being there with her mom and dad. Through everything that had been happening lately, she was talking about both of them with the same level of a loving parent and child relationship. She said it was the first time she'd experienced the kind of peace I had been telling her about. Suddenly it was making sense to her and she wanted to understand more about all of it. I wasn't quite sure what she meant by that. I certainly didn't feel like I understood all of it myself. I told her that was great. It could give her a whole new way of living and being happy.

She enthusiastically responded, "Yes, I see that now. That is why I want you to teach me everything!"

I felt paralyzed. I definitely had not been expecting this. My heart began beating rapidly and I thought I was going to pass out. I never planned on being a mentor/teacher. Ironically, I thought this was what you were supposed to go to priests and ministers for. They were the ones who were the educators; anybody else was a cult leader. I thought I had given her the formula by telling her to meditate, contemplate, and then listen. I thought that was everything a person needed to know. I was wondering if buying another puppy could get me out of this one.

Finally, I responded, "What is it you want to learn and why do you want me to be the one to teach you?"

"I want to learn how to find happiness and I want you to teach me because you are the only person I know who can show and tell. And most of all because" —there was a dramatic pause with a slight head tilt, and tears began to well up in her eyes— "I trust you."

I could not think of any possible scenario where I could say no. She had me at "hello," and that had happened over a year ago.

I told her, "I'm not sure how to do this. There isn't any manual or course to follow."

She responded—and I really hate when people use your own words against you— "You have told me that everybody has a story to tell. Just tell me your story." Then she smiled; she knew she had me.

"I'll have to think about it." I knew I was going to do it but I had to buy some time to figure out how.

"Go meditate and contemplate on it; I have." (Have I said how much I hate when people use your own words against you?!)

"You're such a smart-ass. You already know all that you need to know."

"Maybe I just want to feed an old man's ego," she teased.

"Then we should start soon before I die of old age."

She quickly retorted, "Then we should start tomorrow."

From that point on we got to work an hour earlier every day and stayed at least an hour later on most days for "class." The conversations covered almost every available moment we had. I never realized I had so much to tell.

The hard part for me was figuring out where to start. I didn't want to bore her with useless and uninteresting stories. After spending a lot of time thinking about my course syllabus, I arrived for the first lesson. After about ten minutes of me telling her I didn't know where to begin and how to get started she asked me when the first time was that I thought about God or the answers to the universe.

That was the triggering moment for me. My thoughts immediately took me to my back porch as a little kid staring at the stars with wonderment. I had never put that together with my "Rocky Mountain High" meteor shower experience. It was a moment that validated that I was supposed to be right here doing what I was doing right now with Mack. From then on, I never struggled with what to talk about. I was at peace with the whole situation.

I also found it intriguing that this was nearing the end of July and the yearly passage to my vision quest was just around the corner. When I brought up my Aspen experience to Mack, she was very attentive and asked a lot of questions. She found the whole thing to be very exciting and spiritually invigorating. "Spiritually" was not a term Mack used very often, but I noticed as our conversations went on that the term became a part of her regular vocabulary. Prior to that she had used the word "religious" when referring to God, but now she was replacing it with "spiritual." That was very much the same thing I had done. Overall, we did not talk specifically about God all that much. We tended to talk more about happiness, freedom from the world, and peace. "Peace" was a word that was not easily defined, but once you recognized what it was, you knew when you had it. That was what drove you to find it, and keep it with everything that you did.

As our discussions continued, she referred to the Aspen adventure a lot. She always asked a great deal of questions about my vision quests over the years. She wanted to know what I wished for and what had come true and what my disappointments were. Her eternal assessments of my vision quests started to identify to me patterns and explanations to things that had happened (and were happening) in my life. Things that I had never noticed before were now making a lot of sense to me. These insights, along with our overall lessons, were providing me with a tremendous number of things to write about in my own journal. My story was growing exponentially just by sharing it with Mack. There were all these new addendums to my story.

The pattern that kept presenting itself to me was that my vision quests were my guideposts. They kept me going to my true north, my destination, just like ships use lighthouses to arrive safely into harbor. Telling Mack about my vision quests made me realize that each year my wishes and desires had become more about achieving a destination of peace than about things. When Mack said that out loud to me, it was like I had arrived at my harbor safely. I also started thinking about my last two vision quests in particular. They had been different, more philosophical and introspective. I also thought about how my life had become more that way, and how my relationship with Mack was a barometer for me to see where I was in reference to my inner guide.

The scariest thing of all was that Mack and I were at a place I never thought we would ever be. We were talking about everything. We enjoyed each other and felt lost when we weren't together. She defended me to her family, even to her dad. I didn't know how to define our relationship. We weren't just friends, we weren't lovers, and even the term "best friends" didn't seem adequate. We were both married and we knew we couldn't talk about our relationship with other people because they wouldn't understand. We would never be able to explain to people why this fifty-one-year-old man was hanging around this sexy twenty-something girl. None of this mattered to either of us. All we knew was that what we had was something special.

I don't know what, if anything, she was telling Jessie about us. It wasn't like she was avoiding talking about him, she just had nothing to say. It was like he was non-existent. We did talk about Emily periodically. I never said anything bad or negative about her. Actually, everything I had to say about Emily was about how special she was. I had also gotten to where I wasn't hiding anything about my relationship with Emily and I even talked about how much I loved her. Mack would say how lucky Emily was to have me and how lucky I was to have her. I would always agree.

I started to wonder what was next for Mack and me. We were at a special place for any relationship. But everything always changes, and this would, too. It was the week before my vision quest. Mack's leg was better and she really didn't need me at the store anymore, but that didn't change anything. I was still coming in early and staying late every day. Our conversations were still going strong. We always had something to talk about. One thing about our conversations that started to present itself was how serious or deep they were. We had not had many light or funny moments since they began. On top of that, the store had been very busy, so neither of us had done anything recreational. It was all talk, work, and more talk.

On this particular day, the topic was about past relationships and good and bad dating experiences. Apparently, that is a great topic to change the course of serious and intense conversation. What seemed devastating as a teenager was now outrageously funny. What made it even funnier was that our stories were coming from both sides—the boy and the girl. Each story was funnier than the previous one. We were laughing hysterically and we needed that. It reminded us both that living includes laughing and having fun, not just figuring out the universe.

We stayed a little later than usual that night because we were on a roll. She didn't seem to need to get home and Emily was going out with a friend. As we ran out of laughing gas, the discussion turned to her asking, "If we had been in school together, would you have asked me out?"

"Oh, hell no!"

She looked shocked and a bit befuddled. "Why not?"

"Because you would have been way out of my league. I don't think I could have even talked with you because of how gorgeous you are."

"Aww," she replied. "You are so sweet."

"No, I'm not. I'm just a big chicken who would have been very angry with myself for not having the guts to even talk to you,"

"What if I had asked you out?" she asked.

"Really? You really think that would have ever happened?"

She repeated a quote from a movie I had told her about. "You know, sometimes all you need is twenty seconds of insane courage. Just literally twenty seconds of just embarrassing bravery. And I promise you, something great will come of it." (Have I said how much I hate it when people use my words against me?!)

Then she said, "Some things need to be left a mystery to the universe." But after a moment, she shifted the conversation, "What would you do for a first date with me?"

I repeated her words back to her. "Some things need to be left a mystery to the universe." After I was done laughing, I said, "I would never do anything so normal like a dinner and a movie. That would just be so boring. And why would I want to spend money and give flowers to a girl on a first date if I wasn't sure I would still like her after the date?" Then I asked her, "What would you like to do for a first date?"

"I would like my date to bring me flowers and take me to a nice restaurant and then to a movie." I could tell she was just trying to be difficult.

"It's a good thing we didn't go out, because we would have never made it." We kind of smiled but we never laughed and it was getting late and was time to go home.

It was Tuesday night and I told her that I was going to be leaving a little bit early on Friday and would not be there on Saturday. (As if I had to ask off from a job that really wasn't a job.) It was my vision quest weekend.

The next day we didn't talk much—at least not our normal intimate talk. The store was kind of slow, so it wasn't because we didn't have the time. Something seemed different, but I couldn't put my finger on it. On Thursday, it was the same: friendly but nothing deep or personal. I was starting to think something was wrong. So, I asked her and she just said, "I have a lot on my mind, but everything is fine." As a seasoned old man, I knew that when a woman said everything was fine, it wasn't. But I decided to just let it go and see how things would be the next day. I told her I would not be in early because I had to get my stuff together for my trip. She replied, "That's fine."

When I got to the store the next morning she was in a good mood. That's another thing my years had taught me: women were moody. She remained in a good mood all morning. Around noon, she asked me what time I was planning on leaving and I told her around two. Then it happened. Something I didn't see coming and that caught me completely off guard and left me in shock. She asked, "Can I go with you?"

I had absolutely no idea what to say. It felt like an hour before I could utter the word, "Sure." Instead of asking if it was appropriate for us to do such a thing I just said, "Sure, I would love to have you come with me." I hadn't even thought about what Emily would think or the potential catastrophic implications of this happening and what was even going on. I just said, "Sure."

She instantly said, "Good. Let's go." She had all of her stuff packed and ready to go. We immediately closed the store and hit the road. I didn't even think about the fact that I was going on this adventure with a woman who wasn't my wife. Not that I thought of this as a rendezvous, but I was still a married man. Even after thinking about it, it still felt like the right thing to do.

Chapter 11

THE DRIVE TO MY VISION QUEST DESTINATION TOOK about two hours. For about the first half hour, things were a bit strange. So many thoughts and feelings were racing through my head and I was extremely confused. What had just happened? Where had this come from? How did we ever get to this place in our relationship? It all felt very surreal. I wasn't feeling like this was something bad, even though it had a touch of naughtiness to it. The only anxiety I was having was that I hadn't been able to plan every detail of the trip. But even that didn't seem to matter to me. As we continued driving down the highway, I was becoming calmer by the mile. I started to think about how perfect all of this was. I was going on my vision quest with a beautiful, sexy young lady and I wasn't worried about my wife, or really anything for that matter. How much better could it get? I did wonder if I had enough beer and popcorn to get us both through the weekend.

We were about an hour into the trip and we had only been talking about normal stuff, when I decided to ask her about Jessie. She said they had split up.

My brain hit the brakes! Huh? What?

"Jessie is not a bad guy," she continued, "but after being told what to do by my father and now my husband I finally realized it was my life and I had to take it back. I now understand that marriage is not a contract to give my life away, it is an agreement to love and care for each other and deeply appreciate what is important for both of us. After talking with my father, he got it. He understood and accepted me and put his love and trust in me to help me succeed at something that made me happy—like the store. Jessie did not give me an option, only an ultimatum. That is not love. I understand that now."

Mack went on to say that that was when she called her mom to come and get her because she needed to get away. That was also when she and her mom began to talk. Mack said that for the first time in her life, she had felt close to her mom and that she could tell her the truth about everything that was going on. Her mom was quiet and just let her talk. She never questioned anything that Mack told her. Mack said for being in such a terrible situation it ended up being something great, something she thought she would never have—a relationship with her mom.

It was during that talk with her mom that she told her everything about me. And after all the talking was done her mom told her she was lucky to have someone like me and not to worry about what other people think. "Trust yourself" is what her mom told her. That was when Mack realized how her mother and I were a lot alike.

Then Mack talked about what happened when her dad got involved in the situation. It was hard for him not to think like a dad protecting his daughter. It was hard for him to see beyond the "how things are supposed to be" and trust what the truth actually was. When he finally heard Mack's side of the story, he had to take some time to think about everything. It was during that time that her dad did a lot of soul searching and found the truth. This whole thing was scaring her dad because what had happened between Mack and Jessie was the same thing he would have done when he was younger. Seeing all of this happen to his daughter woke him up. No one should treat Mack like that and that included him. He realized that love was not telling people what to do but supporting them regardless of what they do. That meant trusting Mack and her mother.

After spending time thinking about everything that was happening, he decided to go and talk to Jessie. He was hoping he could impart some of his newfound wisdom to try and help Mack and Jessie work things out. That didn't happen. Instead, he discovered a man (who reminded him of himself) who only cared about himself. He found a man who believed the role of the wife was to care for him, have his children, fix his meals, and do whatever else he determined was to be done. Was this what he wanted for Mack? Mack's dad had always liked Jessie because he was a man's man: a hardworking country boy who knew how to put in a hard day's work and put food on the table. That is what a man, a husband, was supposed to do. Now it was a different story; his daughter was being held captive and wasn't allowed to do the things that made her happy. He realized the hypocrisy of the situation; he had been trying to instill those values in her through his whole life as her father. After his conversation with Jessie, he realized even more the trap Mack was in with her marriage.

Mack said her father then came to her and told her he was sorry for not listening to her and trusting the daughter he was so proud of. Mack said she started to cry and laugh at the same time and told him, "It's still okay to be my daddy." After that they had a long and deep conversation about everything, including me. It was hard for him, but after he opened up to Mack's mom, he finally got it. If Mack trusted me, then he needed to also.

I was stunned. I whispered, "How did you forget to tell me all of this?"

"I didn't think it was important," she laughed, followed by, "What's for dinner?"

We were only about fifteen minutes from arriving at our destination and an idea popped into my head. Our trip had been intense with such serious conversation and I wanted this weekend to be a sort of release. So, I decided to have some fun. I asked Mack, "Will you go out with me?"

She looked at me strangely and her face appeared puzzled. Then it hit her, "Yes, I will go out with you."

I smiled. "There's one of the mysteries of the universe solved." We both laughed.

She asked me what my plan was since we had not agreed earlier on what our favorite kind of dates were. I said I was going to compromise and take her to a special place for dinner. She would soon find out just how special this place was.

I knew of a place in a small town a few miles away that I liked to go to when I was in the area. I thought it would be perfect for this occasion. We parked the car and were walking up to what appeared to be a rundown redneck bar. The windows were all boarded up but you could see inside through the space between the door and the doorjamb. It probably hadn't been painted since . . . well, ever. I believe Mack said something like, "What the hell?!"

We walked in and everyone in the bar stopped talking, turned, and looked at us. Then they all started to laugh and shouted, "Hey, Brad, great to see you again!" I told Mack that I was a regular there. We were then taken to a back room that was set up as a dining area and had the best chicken fried steak in existence.

As we were walking out Mack said to me, "So this was a compromise? What's next?"

"I am going to show you just how much I am willing to compromise for you,"

She replied, "I can't wait."

During our recent conversation about our dating histories I had mentioned to her that my first car date had been . . . what else? A drive-in movie. She told me that she had never been to one. I could not believe that anyone had not been to a drive-in movie. I teased, "That's like saying you have never seen the movie *Grease*!" She did not say anything. I then exclaimed, "Oh my God! You haven't seen *Grease*!" She actually started to turn a bright shade of red. I had it in my head that I was going to take her to the drive-in to keep up with my dating compromise, but when I pulled up to the ticket window, I could not believe what I saw. *Grease* was the featured movie. The universe was really with me tonight!

She could not believe all that was happening. How could I have put all of this together without even knowing she was coming? I just went with it. We had an absolute blast. I had never had so much fun on a date. During the movie I even thought about how I was with a woman who was even sexier than Olivia Newton-John! Maybe birthday wishes do come true, but just take a little longer to materialize. On the way to the campsite, I stopped for gas. While she went to use the restroom, I purchased a cheap bouquet of flowers. When she got back to the car, I gave them to her. She said, "You told me that you don't give flowers on the first date."

"I don't give flowers before I know if I like the girl." Time paused for a moment. This really was starting to feel like an actual date. I was transported back in time, remembering how nervous I got at the end of a date and the anxiety of the goodnight kiss. That was nothing compared to what I was feeling at that moment. It was just supposed to be fun. Why was I so nervous? I hadn't seen this coming.

Something else I hadn't seen coming was the overnight situation. I wasn't going to be able to take her to the door and say good night and leave. And then never see or hear from the girl again. I was going to be with her for the next thirty-six to forty hours without any escape. Now I really did have anxiety and there was no sign of relief coming. We were both being kind of quiet and not saying much. I was too freaked out wondering what she was thinking about. I decided to do what I would normally be doing on this weekend. I drove to the campsite and started to unload the car. Mack asked if we were going to set up the tent. Normally, if it wasn't supposed to rain, I wouldn't set up the tent until the next day. Before I could say anything, she said, "It's not supposed to rain tonight, so why don't we just set it up tomorrow?"

"That sounds like a good idea." We found a nice spot and put our blankets on the ground and began to settle in. She wasn't like Emily was about camping and sleeping outdoors. Mack actually liked it. She told me she used to sleep out in the barn with Sunshine and Lady a lot. She said it made her feel free. She seemed like she was really looking forward to this. I thought I was too, but I was too freaked out by being in this spot to appreciate the moment.

The conversation started out very general. She asked me questions like: Which vision quest had been my favorite? Who had I gone on vision quests with? Had any of my wishes come true? Then, at the same time, we saw our first shooting star. She was so excited! She asked me what I had wished for and I told her it wouldn't come true if I told her. I personally didn't believe in that part of the protocol for wishing on shooting stars, but I couldn't tell her that I had wished she was singing "Hopelessly Devoted to You" like Sandy sang about Danny in the movie. I guess that should have been a hint to me where my mind was starting to go.

It didn't take long for the questions to get deeper. They kind of had a theme that was along the lines of, "How do you think God feels about [insert everything here]?" She told me my answers taught her a lot. She said I was like a conduit for God speaking to her. *Great! Now I am God's interpreter!* Now that is a tough job, and I was pretty sure I did not want that responsibility.

She went on, "What you tell me makes sense in ways the Church, priests, and the Bible can't. It all feels right coming from you, and you not only say it but you also live it. You make it come alive to me." I had absolutely no clue how to respond to that.

Fortunately, the shooting star fireworks really kicked in then. It was one star after another in rapid succession. We spent the rest of the night oohing and ahhing over this spectacular event. It was an answer to one of my wishes to change the subject.

As it got close to dawn, we both drifted off to sleep for a while. You really didn't sleep a lot on these trips because you were up all night and during the day you had to battle the sun. We finally got up and decided to go out for breakfast instead of my usual campfire-cooked eggs. It felt like we just needed some time away from the campsite.

This little town did not have much in the way of sightseeing or shopping, so we were going to have to create our own fun. I'd chosen this town for precisely that reason. These weekends were not supposed to have any distractions so I could focus on my purpose. This year my purpose had changed and there wasn't a new, clear agenda coming to me. I would just have to go with the flow and hope for the best. The problem with that was I did not have the opportunity to separate myself from things when they happened and give myself time and space to sort through them. I had to react in that moment. I wasn't sure I was that strong and had that much control.

The day was pretty normal and I was feeling really good. The high anxiety of the situation was settling down and things were normalizing. It appeared that Mack was feeling that way, too. We stopped at a park that was next to a river and just sat for a while. I don't remember how the conversation got started, but we were talking about how peaceful the weekend was. We both were talking about how the rest of the world had disappeared and there was nothing to think about except for that moment. There were no bills to think about or things we "had" to do. The only thing that mattered was the moment we were in.

At one-point Mack told me that this was what she needed to shoot for and she saw that I was already there. I found her comments to be very rewarding and inspirational. It made me think that the universe was telling me that there really was a purpose behind our relationship. I truly felt I had made a positive impact on Mack's life and that was something I should be proud of. But the thought kept coming to me: "What's next?" I knew that was not consistent with living in the moment but I couldn't help myself. Throughout my whole relationship with Mack I was always searching for what was next. Now, it was different. Before, there were so many different directions things could go but now we were at a place where the road had narrowed. I was feeling somewhat sad and depressed when I thought about that. Was our relationship winding down? Had its purpose been achieved? There was no end destination I could see; or maybe there was and I just didn't want to see it.

I was thinking a lot about all of that heading into the evening. This was the last night of our trip—what was life for us going to be like when we returned home? I had a very strong feeling that it was not going to be the same, but I couldn't tell if that was going to be good or bad. But Mack's words came back to me: "Live and appreciate the moment; that is all that really matters." The student had become the teacher.

I decided to let the evening take its own course. The weather was perfect and we were set for a wonderful night of gazing at the heavens watching shooting stars. I think Mack was having some introspective thoughts, too. Her tone was pleasant and calm and her demeanor very peaceful. The night moved at a comfortable, smooth pace. Our conversation was not deep like the night before but more reflective in nature. My thoughts were taking me to a realization I had not been to in the year and a half I had known Mack. Someone who started out as a clerk in a store selling me kittens and kitty litter was now my soul mate. Had I really just thought that? And what did that even mean, "soul mate"? Other than my birthday kiss there wasn't a sexual component to our relationship, at least not outwardly. But the truth was, there wasn't anyone else in the world I wanted to be with more. Our relationship didn't feel like a marriage, with certain obligations, but the desire to be together and openly share our thoughts and feelings felt so natural. I wanted this moment in time to stop and never start again. This was perfect; this was everything I dreamed peace would be.

What I didn't know was what Mack was thinking. We knew so much about each other now and we were so comfortable, but did she consider me her soul mate? Had she ever heard of the term "soul mate"? After all, she had never been to a drive-in movie or seen *Grease*, so what else didn't she know about? I felt so emotionally full and empty at the same time.

Right in the middle of all this contemplation my thoughts were interrupted by Mack asking, "What are you thinking about right now? And be totally honest with me."

As I had been so many times in my relationship with Mack, I was stunned and shocked at the same time. How was I supposed to answer? How could I not answer? I knew I had to tell her the truth. At that moment the "twenty-seconds of insane courage leading to great things" quote came to mind. It was time for me to jump off that cliff. I went for it. I told her the truth.

When I was done my heart was pounding and I thought I was going to pass out. The following moments of silence felt like hours. There were no more words left in me to speak, so I just waited for her response. We had been lying on our backs looking up at the stars during our conversation. She sat up and turned toward me and looked me straight in the eyes. I thought her eyes were welling up with tears, but it was dark so I wasn't sure. She continued to just look at me for again what seemed to be an eternity, until she leaned over and hugged me.

This was no ordinary hug; it must have lasted at least ten Mississippis. I wanted to cry and jump for joy at the same time but I couldn't do anything except cherish the moment. When she let go, we both lay back down but, in the process, she cuddled up next to me. Her head was on my shoulder, her body pressed up against mine with her hand over my heart. Nothing more was said by either of us. That was how we spent the rest of the night and quietly fell asleep. When I said earlier how things were perfect and I didn't think they could get any better, I was wrong; this was perfection.

When we awoke the next morning, everything was back to normal. We packed up and went out for breakfast like the day before. Within an hour we were on the road headed for home. We didn't talk much, but I wasn't sure if that was because of what had happened or because we were just tired. I knew in my case it was because so many thoughts were racing through my mind. My thoughts also kept going back to the question, *What's next?*

We arrived back at the shop, where Mack had left her pickup truck. We unloaded her stuff and as I went to give her a hug, she put her arms around me and gave me a big kiss on the lips followed by the strongest hug I have ever had. Then she got into her pickup and just drove away. That was not what I had expected to happen. I also didn't expect what happened next to happen, but it did. And I wished it hadn't.

Chapter 12

THE NEXT DAY WAS MONDAY AND MEANT BACK TO THE normal routine. I arrived an hour early like always but I was exceptionally excited to begin our new level of relationship. When Mack didn't show up right away, I wasn't concerned because I just attributed it to the fact that it had been a long weekend and she was probably just getting a little extra sleep; she really wasn't a morning person as I had found out the preceding couple of days. I did start to worry a bit when nine o'clock rolled around and she still wasn't there. Even though she was a slow riser she was never late to work. I waited until about nine thirty, and then I started to worry that something had happened. I hadn't gotten any calls or texts, and that wasn't like Mack when plans got changed.

Then I started to worry that this had something to do with our weekend. Had she thought about everything that had happened and freaked out? I tried calling and sending her texts but there was no answer. I thought about calling her mom, but I was still feeling unsure about where I fit into the family hierarchy. I was really starting to panic. She was my soul mate now and I really sensed something was wrong but I had no idea what to do. I didn't even know where she actually lived! I was completely paralyzed and in shock and fear. I continued to try to call and text but to no avail. The day just continued to go on with me going crazier with each minute. I decided to try and do the only thing I could think of: pray. I was still at the store late in the afternoon when I finally decided to head home. It was a different location, but my panic and fear were still the same.

When Emily got home, she immediately knew something was wrong. When she asked me, I didn't know what to say. Finally, I told her that I thought something had happened to the girl at the store. I had gotten to where I was using Mack's name with Emily; I don't know if it was my guilt from the weekend or what that made me say "the girl at the store." Emily even asked, "Do you mean Mack?" For some strange reason her response made me feel somewhat better. Nothing changed for the remainder of the day. I didn't even come close to getting any sleep that night and it felt like I might not ever get any sleep again.

I kept waiting for eight o'clock in the morning to come so I could go back to the store like normal and hope that this had just been a horrible nightmare. I couldn't make it until eight, so I got there at seven. I couldn't believe it. Mack's pickup truck was there! I could breathe again! It felt like the weight of the world had been lifted off my shoulders. I was so excited to see Mack again and give her a big hug. I jumped out of my car and ran to the shop. I don't even remember opening the door.

When I got there Mack had her back to the door but it was her and that was all that mattered. I said with all the happiness of the world in my voice, "Hey, where have you been? I've been worried about you." Nothing could have ever prepared me for what happened next.

Without even turning around she said in a quiet, angry tone, "Go away. I don't ever want to see you again."

I couldn't believe what I had just heard so I asked her to repeat what she said. This time her tone was no longer quiet, but it was still angry—very angry.

I asked, "What did I do? Why are you so upset?"

She finally turned around and with fire in her eyes yelled, "You ruined my life! You ruined everything! My life was just fine until you came into it and took everything that I loved away from me, and I will never be able to get it back! Just leave!"

I was completely devastated and horrified. "Please tell me what happened," I begged.

She screamed back at me even louder than before, "While you took me to go out and look at stupid stars and make stupid wishes, my daddy had a heart attack... and he died! I wasn't even there to be with him!" She completely broke down sobbing. I started to tell her how sorry I was but before I could finish one word she screamed, "Save it! There is nothing you can say or do to change anything. You can't wish on a shooting star for your dead daddy to come back! JUST GO!"

I stood there for a moment until she caught her breath. Then she seethed, "You know what I wish for? I wish that you would just go away for good! *I wish that you would just go away for good!*"

I knew logically that she didn't really mean that. People say a lot of things out of emotion at such a horrible moment. All I ever wanted was for Mack to be happy and I was the one who ruined that. The only thing I could do was accommodate her wish. Without saying another word, I turned and hoped that her last wish would never come true.

Chapter 13

"I WISH THAT YOU WOULD JUST GO AWAY FOR GOOD!" I didn't know why I said those words. I knew my dad dying was not Brad's fault and I shouldn't have blamed him. Ironically, it was everything he'd taught me that got me through all of it. I didn't know why I blamed it all on him. Maybe it was because he was the only person I could trust enough to take my anger out on. Maybe it was because he made me feel so good and I didn't want to feel good. I don't know, but I guess it didn't really matter anymore; it was over. I wanted to call him and say I was sorry but I couldn't, and I didn't know why. I was hoping he would show up at the funeral, but he didn't. I knew he was just respecting my "wish" but it just gave me another reason to justify my anger at him. I continued to go into work an hour early every morning, expecting him to be there, but he wasn't. Even if he had been, I was pretty sure I would have continued to vent my rage at him.

The customers always asked about him and I didn't know what to say, so I just told them he got another job, even though he didn't even work for me in the first place. Everyone seemed disappointed he was gone. I'd never realized how popular he was with all the customers. They all told me a story about conversations they had with him, followed by a laugh or a shake of their heads while saying things like, "I'd never thought about it that way." Some of the customers told me that the reason they first visited the store was because of him. He would start up a conversation with them and talk about this wonderful store they had to visit. He made it sound so appealing that they just couldn't say no. Every one of these customers would tell me to give Brad well wishes when I saw him. I tried to put on a brave face whenever these conversations came up but each time made the store feel empty without him. It made me feel empty, too.

I never realized just how big a part of my life he actually was. I didn't even know how we got to be the way we were, or for that matter *what* we were. All I knew was that I missed him. He was my soul mate. Before I met him, I didn't even know what a soul mate was. Now I couldn't imagine a life without one, especially him.

Oddly enough, I could remember the first time he came into the store. I hadn't been in business very long and didn't have many customers. That made it easier to remember the ones I did have. I remembered him because he was kind of cute in a different way. He was older but I couldn't tell you how old he actually was. He had a kind of childlike presence to him. I felt comfortable with him from the start. He seemed lost and not sure of the reason he was even in the store. He bought flowers for his mom every week, so I knew he had to be a nice guy. Plus, I was excited about having a return customer, period. It didn't take long for me to start looking forward to him stopping by. I had trouble remembering his name and it seemed to annoy him, but I thought it was kind of cute, so I had some fun with it. At first, he didn't talk very much but he would always smile and say "please" and "thank you." You would think that should be the norm in society, but it was quite the opposite. However, it made him stick out and catch my attention.

After several weeks of him purchasing flowers for his mom, I started thinking this was just too good to be true. My suspicion played out when he came to the store one week and told me his mom had enough flowers and she was becoming overwhelmed caring for them. Then, I really started to think about him when he adopted a kitten. He really did not look like he was in the market for a kitten. He said he always wanted a pet but never had one. I told him, "You aren't getting any younger." Looking back, that comment probably did not help with his state of mind about his age. He ended up taking the kitten along with anything I had in the store related to kittens. I had to laugh (on the inside) because he was so cute and unmanly. Still, I wouldn't have given him the kitten if I didn't think he would make a good pet parent, and I just knew in my gut he would take great care of his new best friend.

When I told my husband, Jessie, about Brad, he told me right away that this guy had a crush on me. Jessie told me he would take care of this "creepy old man" and I told him that I could take care of myself. Nothing more about it was said between Jessie and me, but it did get me to start thinking. I had been told on several occasions that I was "cute" and "hot" and a number of other terms that I deemed to be inappropriate. I had just learned to smile and move on. Brad was different.

He didn't try to hide the fact that he was married. He wore his wedding ring and would periodically mention his wife. He never made any lewd comments or sexual innuendos or the intentional unintentional touch. He never asked me out or to have sex; he didn't even undress me with his eyes. I honestly never thought there was that kind of attraction going on, but now that I was thinking about it, I kind of liked it. As I continued to contemplate this line of thinking—and I had plenty of time between customers to do a lot of thinking—my thoughts turned from a cute older man crush to, *What is love and attraction all about?* Over time, I felt good about how Brad and I interacted, but it also made me think about how Jessie and I interacted.

I met Jessie while I was going to community college. He was the brother of the boyfriend of a girl I met in class. I wasn't really looking to date anyone since I was so busy with school and work. It simply started out as someone to keep me company when a group of us would go out on a Friday or Saturday night. There really was no special "connection" but he was nice and cute in a rugged sort of way. He was like my dad, in that he could fix just about anything, and he was always busy. He had his main job working as an electrician, but he was also working a lot of side jobs to put money away. He was big on security and having money for a rainy day. I suppose those were good qualities for a husband, right?

We had dated for about a year when he asked me to marry him. I remember thinking it was the next thing to do after school, you know: school, marriage, kids, housewife and mother. I was just twenty-two when we tied the knot. I had no idea what I really wanted to do with my life; I didn't even understand what the options were. I didn't know I wanted to run my own business at that time, but I knew I wanted to do something other than just sit around. Jessie sold me on the idea that I could be a housewife and do something with horses. That was good enough for me. Kids weren't discussed much, just that neither of us seemed interested in them. I was good with kids as long as they went home with someone else after about an hour. The relationship between Jessie and me seemed to be what everybody thought a marriage should be. We were a cute couple in everyone else's eyes. I accepted that perspective until I started to look at it through my own eyes.

It was not unusual for store owners and their customers to have regular conversations and get to know each other some, but this felt different. I couldn't say why, but it just was. I had worked my way through college as a waitress and I had many regulars who I would call my friends, but I was discovering that the definition of the word "friend" had many different meanings. Up until that point, I had used that word to describe anyone whose name I knew and with whom I could exchange a pleasant salutation and maybe even a short conversation . . . a noun.

With Brad it was different. It had a feeling behind it, like a verb. Finally, I had an experience with a dictionary that actually taught me something. Brad introduced me to a whole new level I hadn't seen before. Most of the male "friends" I had were a result of the cat-and-mouse game, where I would smile and tilt my head and they would reciprocate their devotion by giving me a bigger tip. I learned to smile and tilt my head a lot. I also felt like they expected me to be my best, if you know what I mean, for that price. But between waitressing, school, and my real true loves, Sunshine and Lady, there hadn't been much time to date. I would spend every available moment and some moments that weren't available with Sunshine and Lady. I would study out in the barn with them, and many nights I would fall asleep in the hay.

It didn't seem to matter anyway. Anytime I was asked out it was usually only a one-and-done. That was either because my dad was John Wayne reincarnated standing at the door waiting to greet my suitor before, and at the end of my date, or the date realized that I could kick their ass if there was any difference of opinion of the night's agenda. You see, I had kind of a reputation growing up. My dad wanted a boy to raise in his image, but he got me instead. He pretended I was a boy and taught me all the things he'd planned to teach his son. I could shoot, drive a tractor, and do all the chores any boy could do and do them even better. Because of this, somewhere along the way, my name went from Mackenzie to Mack. My dad said it was because I was like a Mack Truck and nothing could stop me. I thought it was pretty cool, so I went along with it; however, with the title came some repercussions. Boys were often afraid of me. That was okay up until the point I wanted to go out on a date. I also struggled with an identity crisis. I grew up not really liking all of the foofy-type stuff that girls traditionally liked. I was happier cleaning stalls and bailing hay. I knew this made my dad happy on several fronts, but I was still a girl and slowly I was giving in to all that went with that.

I only had one real relationship. It lasted about ten months and that was only because it was convenient for me to have someone to do things with when I needed it. Well, I was twenty, drunk, and behind all my friends in the having-sex competition. So, I took the opportunity to catch up because I thought it was what you were supposed to do. It was one of the worst days of my life. I learned a lot from that experience. Don't drink too much and don't get talked into having sex just because everybody else is doing it. It wasn't what I thought, or what people told me, the experience would be. I felt I had let my mom, my dad, and myself down. After that I buckled down and totally dedicated myself to finishing school. I didn't have sex again until I met the man I married. And that experience wasn't any better.

Originally, I was going to school to be a veterinarian, but it didn't take me long to realize that I didn't have the money or the stamina to make that happen, so I shifted gears. I still wanted to work with animals and I was interested in healthy eating so I combined those interests and went into animal nutrition. I worked hard and got my degree. It was only an associate's degree, but for someone who wasn't a great student it felt fantastic. But that feeling did not last very long. A degree does not mean much if it doesn't get you a job. It was a very difficult time for me, but I needed to work doing something. I had worked at a local stable since my early teens and I was still helping out when I could. I was put in charge of ordering the food and feeding all of the animals so I could at least say I was getting something to put on my résumé. I didn't think much about it other than it was a job and it was around horses and other animals. It was a little bit of money to help me buy some time. I had never been driven by money, but a girl still had to make a living.

As time went on, people were starting to ask me questions about healthy diets for their horses and then their other pets. I was increasingly buying more products in bulk and selling to the clients. The word of mouth started to spread, bringing in more business. It wasn't long before it was taking up so much time that I wasn't able to do my other tasks. My dad came to me with the idea of opening a store and expanding into some other things. I think he always wanted to have a business of his own, but he was too afraid of failing to provide for the family. He had worked for only one company his entire life. It was a good living, but we weren't rich. Still, we never really wanted for anything. Maybe it didn't matter because we were simple folk, I guess you would say. Neither of us knew anything about running a business but the idea did pique my interest. Little by little his encouragement convinced me to give it a try. He said, "Mack"—which is what he called me when I was in his son mode— "there is nothing that can stop you if you put your mind and heart into it; you're like a Mack Truck at full throttle." My dad offered me some money he had put away for his retirement and would not take no for an answer when I tried to refuse. Once he knew I wanted to do this, he wasn't going to let anything get in the way. That's just how he was.

It all came together fast. It was like the universe was clearing the path for us. I fell in love with this small roadside farm stand that had been empty for a couple of years. The rent was affordable and it needed very little work to get into store condition. Within a month, the store was up and running. That was the easy part. We had to learn what we didn't know and then learn how to do that. There was insurance, inventory, advertising, taxes (city, state, and local), along with building codes and zoning regulations. What had I gotten myself into? Was this whole thing a bad idea and going to ruin our lives? I was failing before I even got started and I was taking Dad down with me. My dad never said much but he sat me down and simply said, "Rev it up, Mack. We got a trip to take." I had to show my dad I could do this; failure was not an option. He believed in me and it was time for me to believe in me, too.

It started off slowly and continued slowly for what seemed like forever, but then people started to stop by. Each week, a few more customers would come by and there were even some customers who came back. I wasn't making much money, but I didn't need much to survive either. As the weeks went by, my knowledge and understanding of running a business was growing. My confidence was also growing, making me more comfortable dealing with the customers. I realized that smiling and tilting my head at the customer didn't work as well as it had when I was a waitress.

Brad was a stabilizing factor for me during the early days of the business. He didn't come into the store because he knew me and was just supporting a friend of the family. He came into the store to buy something for real and he was coming back because he wanted to and not because he felt obligated to. His weekly visits and our friendly conversations were calming my anxieties and it was helping me settle into my new life.

Brad had a good sense of humor. He used to say that he could not figure out what kind of store this was, but that was one of the things he liked about it. He kept encouraging me to keep people guessing. He was always telling me that I was doing a good job and to trust my gut. The gut was God's greatest gift to us and we should use it. When he kept coming back for the flowers for his mom, I thought it was a bit unusual, but I like unusual; plus, I liked his company. I have to admit that the day he came in and said his mom didn't want flowers anymore, I started to panic. I thought he was coming in to say good-bye, and it wasn't losing a customer that scared me; it was losing my new friend who I barely knew.

Subconsciously, I think I knew he adopted the kitten to help me out, but I wasn't ready to go there. I decided to give myself some credit as a terrific salesperson. Even though I said that tilting my head while smiling wasn't working as well as it had when I was a waitress, it did work pretty well on Brad. I did have to throw in a flip of the hair to seal the deal though.

Chapter 14

BRAD HAD A NEW REASON TO STOP BY THE STORE EV-ery week and I was strangely happy about that. The interactions between us continued to become more comfortable and natural. His new furry friend gave us a new upbeat topic to talk about each week. He told me every little thing this kitten did with such an expression of excitement that I found him more interesting than the stories themselves. I had never experienced anything like this with any of the men I had ever known. He would just keep going and going and I would just listen and smile. It was always a precious moment that would continue until the next customer came in. He would become embarrassed when he realized that he had been talking so much, and he would blush and say he'd better be going. This routine continued for weeks to come.

Eventually, those conversations began to turn to other things. He started asking me about my business and why I became an entrepreneur. He wanted to know if owning my own business made me happy. I had never really thought about it, but when I did, I realized I was happy. It also made me realize that Jessie had never asked me that. He let me know that he wasn't happy about it, but he would say that if it made me happy that is what mattered. I knew that sounded supportive but it never felt that way.

When I asked Brad about what he did for a living, he would only tell me that he'd worked in corporate America for many years until he could no longer tolerate it. It was a while before he ever went into any details about pursuing his interest in writing. He seemed like he was uncomfortable with the status of not having a "real" job and being the family provider. I had to admit I was not sure if this was a good or bad thing. It was another thing that I had never experienced with the men in my life. Eventually, I found it was the simplicity and the courage to follow a passion that appealed to me instead of the drive to chase money. I started thinking about Jessie working so hard for security and status and I would wonder if it was all worth it in the end. For Jessie, it was more important for him to work and provide for the family so I wouldn't have to, but it was at the expense of allowing me to do what made me happy. That was what made sense to him, but he'd never asked what I wanted.

I thought things were going well but it seemed like Brad began talking less as the weeks went by. I was not very good at asking people personal questions, especially when I didn't know them very well, but I mustered up some courage and asked him if everything was alright. He told me that he was feeling down because his kitten was growing up and not doing all those cute kitten things anymore. I really hadn't expected that answer but I don't think I believed it either. Most of the guys I knew had more fun letting their hunting dogs chase the cats. But his comment was the kind of thing that made him special to me. In an attempt to cheer him up, I went and got another kitten I had and told him that all he needed to do was to adopt another one to keep the first one company. I thought I was being funny, but he exclaimed, "That's a great idea!" He took the kitten. I still didn't believe that that was the real reason for his mood, but it didn't matter to me whether he was taking the kitten because he decided he loved cats or he was just trying to support me. He was somebody special.

His mood did pick up after that and our conversations were becoming lighthearted and fun. He had a way of using humor that was not attacking or mean, which was the kind of bar-room humor I was used to. I was continuing to call him by different names every time he came into the store, but I was running out of new names. I was pretty sure he knew I was joking but the joke finally ran its course.

One day he came into the store and I didn't recognize him at first. He looked like a greeter at Walmart. He was wearing a baseball cap and some sort of sticker on his shirt. He got his stuff and came up to the counter, acting totally normal. By that time, I could see more clearly what he was wearing. The sticker on his shirt was one of those that said, "Hello my name is Brad." The hat he was wearing had "Brad" stitched across the front. I had never seen him be so outrageous before and I broke into laughter and was heading for tears.

That is when Jessie came into the store. He very rarely came to the store and this was totally unexpected. Not that it should have mattered, but it did. Brad and I never really talked about our families very much. I did know that he was married and his wife was an accountant but that was about it. I had never said anything to him about Jessie or even about being married. It just never came up.

Jessie wasn't a bad guy. As a matter of fact, in my world he was considered a real good kind of guy. He was a big, strong country boy with an uncompromising work ethic. He had a good job and worked to provide for his family and went drinking with the boys on Friday nights. He was a man's man, which meant being the head of the household—dictating the family rule was his job description. He was the kind of guy every father wants his daughter to marry and every girl wants to capture, in my world anyway. But that was the only world I knew. It was my own fault that I hadn't been paying more attention to what was going on around me during the time Jessie and I were dating. It had all seemed so normal the way everything was happening. That was how it was happening for all my friends and was even the way life went on in my own family with my mom and dad.

Looking back, it was all so scripted and all we had to do was read the lines and act the parts. There was no room to question if it was right or wrong; it was just the way it was and I played my role. But my world was changing, and I was seeing things through a whole new set of eyes. And it was on that day in the store that my vision became much clearer.

On the surface, it should not have been any big deal when Jessie walked into the store. For all intents and purposes, the marriage between Jessie and me was fine, and in theory there wasn't really any kind of relationship other than store owner and customer between Brad and me. But it quickly became clear that this went deeper than the surface. When Jessie walked into the store everything stopped. I had been laughing harder than I had in a very, very long time and Brad was laughing with me. We both just stopped. An awkward few moments went by when I did the only thing I could: I introduced my husband, Jessie, to Brad. There was no manly handshake or even a cordial smile. Brad seemed shocked and stood in silence. Jessie nodded his head and said "hi." He then paused and looked down at Brad's name tag and said, "Brad." It had been a long time since Jessie and I had had the conversation about the "creepy old man" in the store and nothing had been spoken about it since, but Jessie knew who this creepy old man was and he knew that I knew he knew.

I could tell by the look on Brad's face that Jessie had just said something inappropriate, but I was so lost in my own head that I didn't hear what he said. So, I just finished ringing up the sale and said, "Have a nice day." Brad responded with the same and acknowledged Jessie in doing so. I cannot accurately describe how I was feeling at that moment, but I can tell you that it wasn't good. I was angry and upset, not with anyone but myself. I knew I had hurt Brad and it made me feel horrible, but I didn't know why or at least I would not admit it to myself. I was angry with myself because I had not been honest with Jessie or myself about what I was feeling. That was not on Jessie; that was on me. Jessie stayed for just a few minutes after Brad left and when he walked out the door, I put the closed sign up, locked the door, and went into the back and cried. I didn't know why but I had to find out for myself so this wouldn't happen again. I then thought I might never see Brad again. I started to cry yet once more.

I was ready to have it out with Jessie when I got home that night. This had to be his fault, right? I was right, and I was ready to fight this battle as I headed for the door. I walked in and Jessie was in the kitchen. He turned to me and said in a very sincere, heartfelt voice, "I'm sorry. I wasn't very friendly with your customer today. I don't know why I acted the way that I did but I was wrong. Please tell him I apologize for the way I acted and if there is anything I can do to make it up to him just let me know." Jessie had also made my favorite dinner and continued to pamper me and treat me like a queen, something he had not done in a very, very long time. He continued to be sweet and caring for several days and things went well, at least status-quo well for a while.

It was almost a month after that event that Brad came back to the store. I couldn't look him in the eye or even say I was sorry. Moreover, I couldn't tell him that Jessie had apologized. Brad didn't bring it up either. I knew he wasn't saying anything because he knew how horrible I felt and he didn't want me to relive the whole thing or make me explain anything. Besides, the more I got to know him, the more amazed I was at the way he dealt with life. Nothing seemed to rattle him. I wasn't sure why he came back to the store, but that didn't matter; he was back. He said he had gone away for a while and took some time for himself. I used to think that was kind of a "hippie" thing, but all of a sudden it seemed like a good thing. Our relationship took a big step backward for quite a long time, but he kept coming into the store. We could only talk in general terms, but I was grateful for that. I called him Brad from then on.

In the months that followed things continued to be about the same. Brad came to the store every week and got his stuff like any other customer. He was always friendly and pleasant. I never did see Brad with an attitude. Ever. Some weeks he would come and get what he needed and head home; other weeks he would stop and chat for a while. Nothing too deep, though. But then there were those few times something deeper did occur. He would do something beyond the norm—a small gift, some candy or book, cards with sayings that meant something and connected with me. He would say the art of card giving was becoming extinct. He said his mom took giving cards to people very seriously. You didn't give someone just any card, it had to be the perfect card. The card needed to communicate the truth of what was in your heart to them so they would know how much you really cared for them. He said that as he grew up it became important to him that he put the same effort into the cards he gave to her as she did for him. He could always see how much that meant to her. It made such an impact on him that he went on to take the extra effort whenever he got anyone a card. That made the cards he gave to me so much more meaningful because I knew it spoke the truth in a way that did not have to be verbalized or cross the lines of the boundaries our relationship had developed. But then something happened that I wasn't expecting: Valentine's Day.

Even though we had continued to talk over the past months we still had not regained that special "connection" we once had. I think we both felt that connection had been severed by the real world and I believed that whatever Brad's interest had been in me was over. But he was a nice guy and it was okay to just be friends—as in the noun. I had come to the realization that it was out of my control. This was just what it was going to be from now on. But something seemed different that day. There was a certain intensity in Brad's face.

I was working in the store like every other day, and I didn't even realize that it was this hallowed day of love. As I was putting things on the shelf, Brad came in. I was confused because this wasn't his normal stop day; what was he doing here? He walked up to me and said, "I want to adopt that puppy."

I remember thinking, *Am I in a different universe?* Was this really Brad or was I hallucinating? He liked cats, right? He said he needed a change so he thought Emily would really like a puppy for Valentine's Day. All of a sudden, it hit me that it was Valentine's Day. It had never really been an important day for me. Like I have said, I never really dated much and I was not known as a romantic kind of girl, nor did I ever have a romantic kind of boyfriend, or husband, for that matter. All of a sudden, I felt that "loving feeling" people talked about. I was a bit awed and pissed off at the same time. Emily was getting a puppy; that was a sweet gift of love and devotion. *Nobody ever got me a puppy,* I thought angrily. But then I remembered that I never gave anyone a puppy either. But oh, hell, I'm the girl, right?! Should I go and get something for Jessie? He usually spent a lot of money at the grocery store buying me half-dead roses and a box of chocolates I never ate. I guess he tried, at least. For the first time in my life, I was depressed on Valentine's Day. I wanted to have the Valentine's Day experience. I wanted to be Emily.

After we got all the puppy stuff together, I helped carry it all out to Brad's car. When I got back in the store the tears just unloaded, but I had to stop suddenly because Brad was walking back into the store. I asked him if he had forgotten something and he said, "Yes, I did." He handed me a bag and then said, "Have a nice day," smiled, and walked out. I stood there confused for a moment and then looked in the bag. There was a cup of hot chocolate, a can of whipped cream, and a jar of cherries. I started to tremble and the tears began to flow again. This time was for a different reason; I had just had the Valentine's experience.

Keeping in tune with how Brad and I dealt with these "unique" situations, we never discussed it, but I never stopped thinking about it. That day had a major impact on me; I really started to see things differently. I had experienced a feeling I never had before, and I liked it. I wanted to feel that way again. I wondered if I ever would. I decided at that moment that I would not give up seeking that feeling that I previously never knew existed. Now I knew. The next question I asked myself was, "How do I find it?" This feeling had eluded me my entire life until I met Brad. My instincts told me to go to the source and that source was Brad. I had to laugh when I thought, *May the source be with you.* That was a paraphrase right out of Brad's generation, but it made me laugh. That was something I hadn't done in a long time and it felt good. Then it struck me that this was the second time I could attribute my feeling so good to Brad. I was starting to think the universe was sending me a message. Maybe I needed to wish upon a star to find my Valentine.

Chapter 15

I CAN POINT TO THAT VALENTINE'S DAY IN THE STORE as the most pivotal moment in my life up until then. I had decided I would pursue true and real love. I knew what to look for now so I would know when I found it. I hadn't been able to do that before. Brad's gifts to me were truly from the heart and not just out of obligation; they were real. He didn't have to, and he did it with no expectation of anything in return. For the first time in my life, I wanted to give something in return because I wanted to and not because I felt like I should. But wasn't Valentine's Day for lovers? Brad and I weren't lovers and I could not see a world in which we ever would be. Yet, he was the one who got my heart racing. Was that simply by default because of proximity or was there a real connection? Either way, my experience was real and I could not stop thinking about it. I wanted to give a gift to Brad that would mean as much to him as the gift he'd given me had meant. But it had to be the right gift at the right time. I would just have to trust my gut to tell me the what and the when. In the meantime, I still had to go home and deal with my husband and Valentine's Day.

I had not gotten him anything and I was torn between just getting him something and getting through the day or playing it out for real. In hindsight, I probably should have gotten something for him to get through the day and deal with reality later, but I didn't. When I got home, Jessie wasn't there yet so I started dinner. I decided to make a nice steak dinner as a bit of a buffer on the V-Day-gift thing. At least I could play it off as an attempt at doing something special. When he arrived home, he had the usual flowers and candy but there was no card. Not that it should have mattered, but it did. I couldn't even say if he had gotten me any cards in the past, but now I felt like he didn't even care enough to express his feelings for me in Hallmark language. I hadn't gotten him a card either, but my justification to myself was that was that I didn't know what sentiment I wanted to share. Suddenly, I realized truth mattered to me. I was looking for every opportunity to satisfy my discontent by blaming Jessie, even though he didn't deserve it.

After the incident in the store when Jessie treated Brad with attitude and apologized to me and then treated me like a princess for weeks after, things in my marriage went back into a stagnate and meaningless existence. Not bad, not good, just there. We never fought but we also never laughed. Every day was the same boring status quo. That had been accepted because that was the norm in the lifestyle we had grown up in and lived. We hadn't known any differently. But now I did know and that was going to cause a problem. The change started that night on Valentine's Day.

He handed me my "gifts" and gave me the normal hollow kiss. We sat down for dinner and went through the whole meal without saying a word. There were a few uncomfortable glances, but nothing was said. When dinner was over, I picked up the dishes and put them in the dishwasher. I then joined him in the living room for a night of watching mindless TV. That had become our normal evening routine and why would it be any different tonight? Except tonight it was different, at least for me. Every show that night dealt with the highs and lows of Valentine's Day. Each episode drove home how much I had missed over the years and that there was no hope of that changing for the rest of my life unless I did something about it. Again, I asked myself, "But how?" We went the rest of the night saying very little and then joined each other in bed at around nine thirty. He quickly fell asleep while I laid there depressed, asking myself over and over how I was going to find that feeling of love again.

The days that followed were not quite the same normal, lifeless status quo. Feelings were beginning to emerge. But they were not good feelings. They were feelings of frustration, anger, and growing discontent. Tension was growing along with my negative attitude and my passive-aggressive behavior. It finally boiled over when Friday night came and Jessie was getting ready to go out on his weekly rendezvous with his beer-drinking buddies. I started acting out after I realized he was more excited about his Friday nights with the boys than he was about me on Valentine's Day. Finally, the volcano erupted. He lashed out about how I had been acting and how he couldn't do any-thing right. I responded by saying he could drop the "I can't do anything right" act! I don't clearly remember all the words that were shouted after that but I do remember that it ended with him storming out. He didn't come home until two thirty, after closing time. I pretended to be asleep, but I am sure he knew that I wasn't.

Logically, I knew everything that was going on was my fault. I was creating this environment of anger and fury, but this wasn't about being logical; it was about emotions and mat-ters of the heart. I was learning that there was no way to teach how to "love" each other and share intimacy in meaningful ways. But Jessie and I couldn't talk—at least to the degree that needed to be reached. It was much easier to push him away instead so I wouldn't even have to try to have a meaningful conversation. I wasn't ready for that yet. I wasn't sure about everything I was feeling, so how could I talk to him about it?

Things continued to get more contentious and life around home was always tense. I didn't care because, well, I just didn't care. The thoughts I was putting my energy into had to do with finding a way to experiencing that feeling I'd had with Brad on Valentine's Day. I was trying to visualize that feeling without it being Brad, but I hadn't figured out how to do that. Still, things between Jessie and me continued to go downhill and neither of us seemed to care.

The experience on Valentine's Day seemed to reset my rela-tionship with Brad. Our conversations returned to where they had been before. We were laughing and joking consistently again, even more so than before. There were several new things that I noticed about Brad's visits that hadn't previously been apparent. I was carefully planning my wardrobe for the days Brad usually came to the store. I was like a teenager trying to impress a boy in high school—I think. I'm not sure because I was never that girl. I also noticed on those days that I was constantly watching for him and anxiously waiting for him to arrive. When he did arrive, my heart would start to pound faster and I started having trouble coming up with things to say that didn't sound stupid. Once he was there for a while, I would settle down some and relax a bit. His visits started to be more than coming in and getting what he needed and leaving; he would now hang around and linger longer. He would wait until the other customers would leave so we could continue our conversations. Those days and the anticipation of those days were making my other life more bearable. I had moments to live for and they made me feel happy.

One day I had a heavy dose of anxiety but it wasn't because Brad was coming; Jessie was going to be there, too. I had no idea what to expect. Nothing had ever been said between Brad and me about the last time they met but it had manifested in a way that caused our relationship to change. I didn't want that to happen again. We had just re-established our connection. I was hoping something would happen to derail this potential collision course. I was more concerned about the possible negative consequences this could have between Brad and me than I was about the effect on Jessie and me. Actually, my hope was that the consequences would be the impetus to drive Jessie away for good.

When Brad got to the store that day, I wanted to go right up to him and give him a big kiss on the lips right in front of Jessie. Maybe that would be enough to chase Jessie away. The truth of the matter was that Jessie would end up giving Brad a country boy lashing and I would never see Brad again. However, the idea of kissing Brad stuck around in my head. It was the first time there was the thought of physical intimacy with Brad.

Much to my relief and surprise, nothing did happen. Their reunion was uneventful and I was relieved—things could continue on with Brad. I was not sure if Jessie did not recognize Brad from before or if he just didn't care. I knew, though, that Brad did recognize Jessie. I even became cocky by kind of playing around with Brad. Probably trying to force that impetus. I must have called Brad by his name at least four times, each time with a wink and a smile. He would just look at me like, *What the hell are you doing?* and then shake his head and smile. Again, nothing more was ever said. I was having fun and that didn't happen much, only when I was around Brad. He made me feel good.

A few weeks had gone by, but I was still thinking about how to give Brad his Valentine's gift. I wanted it to be special and from the heart; I wanted it to be real. I finally started to come up with an idea after one of Brad's visits. He was acting goofy, even for him, and was talking about all this horoscope stuff. He was trying to be sly about asking when my birthday was. It made me start thinking about when *his* birthday was. So, I took a shot and looked him up on Facebook and was surprised he even had a page. Brad was not very tech savvy, but he claimed he knew enough to be dangerous. Sure enough, his birthday was there, and it was coming up soon. That would be the perfect time; now, all I needed was the perfect "what." I always kind of suspected that Brad was sensitive about his age. There was quite an age difference between us, which I think maybe made him feel uncomfortable. For me though, age was just a number—at least when it came to friendship. As I was thinking that, my thoughts started doing a double-take, wondering if that number did make a difference when it came to a different kind of friendship. That thought was fleeting because I still was not acknowledging that our relationship was anything different from a friendship.

For fun, I decided to look up my horoscope for that day and it said, "Do not put things off because time is precious, but know that truth is more precious than time." All of a sudden, I went from being in a light, easygoing mood to a deep and thoughtful state of mind. I knew right away that this was a message I was supposed to hear; my gut told me so. But from a horoscope?! Really?! I started to dissect the words and what stood out to me was the word "truth." What is truth? More specifically, what is my truth? The first and only thing that came to my mind was that Brad made me happy.

Then, my thoughts shifted to the words "time is precious." Almost immediately I got my message; if I knew what made me happy, why was I wasting my time being unhappy? I couldn't come up with any answer. I also couldn't stop trying. I put it all together and it came out that I shouldn't be afraid to go after Brad because he made me happy and I shouldn't wait. I should do it now because "time is precious." How could I go after Brad? He was married (and happily), he was old enough to be my dad, and would he even want to be with me? How could

I do anything now? I was married (even though unhappily), I was running a business, and how could I explain any of this to my family? Especially my dad! None of this made any sense to me but I also couldn't let it go. The more I tried to not think about it the more pronounced the thoughts became. Adding to the situation, Brad's birthday was coming up fast. I had to come up with something and it had to be good. I battled within myself whether it should be funny or serious, a big deal or just matter-of-fact. I finally decided to tell myself to just relax and take it one step at a time and trust myself to do the right thing. So that is what I kept telling myself I was doing.

It so happened that his birthday fell on the day he regularly stopped at the store. So, I planned for a little surprise party at the store that day. I put the closed sign up because I knew he wouldn't pay attention to that and would come in anyway. The lock on the door was set so when the door closed behind him it would automatically lock. I left King Bayer at home that day so he wouldn't be a headache. When I saw Brad's car pull up, I went and hid in the office in the back. He had never gone back there, but I was pretty sure he would go looking for me since my truck was there and I wasn't. I knew he would worry that something had happened because that was just how he was. If he didn't find me, I rationalized, it just wasn't meant to be.

But I guess it was meant to be because everything happened just as planned, at least for the most part. The part where there was a happy birthday balloon and one of those large chocolate-chip cookies with as many candles as I could put on it was planned. But there was a part that wasn't planned—at least I didn't think it was. When he walked into the back-room office

I jumped up and yelled with excitement, "Happy Birthday, Bert!!!" Then without even thinking about it, I ran up to him and jumped into his arms and kissed him. It was not just any kind of kiss—it was a full tongue-on-tongue-action kind of kiss. I had no idea where that came from and it was something like I had never done before, but I just went for it. While the kiss was happening, I was in a place I had never been before, and I didn't want to leave. It felt so natural and honest. It was even better than my Valentines experience. Then my brain returned to reality and shock set in. But that didn't last long. Within seconds, the smile and enthusiasm returned to my face and I acted just like I felt: happy.

I didn't have to wonder how Brad felt because it was quite obvious: shocked. He didn't freak out or anything like that—actually, quite the opposite. After his moment of shock moved on, he acted like his normal self. At a later time, he told me that his response was because he had no idea of where to go with that moment. He was speechless, like he just won the billion-dollar lottery. The rest of the party was surprisingly normal and uneventful. When he left, I just gave him a hug; I thought anything more would have been a little over the top.

Chapter 16

IN THE WEEKS THAT FOLLOWED, EVERYTHING WAS pretty normal. We didn't talk about what happened, probably because we were both still trying to figure out what really *did* happen. However, Brad was coming to the store more often and hanging around longer. It was coming into spring so there was a lot to do and business was picking up. Brad was actually starting to participate at the store. That's another way of saying he was working at the store but not getting paid. He had plenty of retail experience to teach me and helped grow the store significantly. He did it in ways that did not intrude on my being the boss. He always gave me praise and all the credit for everything good that was happening. He would tell me how proud he was of me. Quite different from what Jessie would say, which was nothing.

After the Valentine's Day experience, this was the next major pivotal moment in my life. Although Brad and I were not in a "couples" relationship, the kiss made me feel like I had never felt before. I asked myself some big questions: Is this what love really feels like? Am I in love with Brad or are my feelings about Brad just by default because he was the one who was there? I knew better but I was still trying to find a way to avoid acknowledging my true feelings. I just couldn't go there. But I knew there was one place I did have to go and that was home.

I never felt guilty about the kiss nor did I ever consider what happened as cheating. To me, it was about discovering truth. I now know that the truth was I did not love Jessie. That didn't mean I knew if I loved Brad but I noted the difference in my heart. I decided I could no longer be with Jessie because that would be a lie. I wasn't blaming Jessie because I understood that all of this was not his fault. It was more my fault for not understanding all of this until now. The only way things could have ever worked out between Jessie and me was if we both understood life and love and connected on that level. Neither of us understood that we would never find peace and happiness in our lives together. In learning and understanding all of that, I realized that most other people don't get it either. That makes for a very lonely place for those who do get it. I know it is possible to coexist with someone you get along with but that does not mean you have that special intimate connection. My observation was that it really couldn't be explained—it had to be experienced. And how did that happen? I didn't know, but I did know that I had to try to explain it all to Jessie.

My life was about to become extremely complicated. Everything was going to change and change was something that was not well accepted in my life circles. It was in my DNA that change was not a good thing and should be avoided at all costs. But I now saw change as something that had to happen if I was ever going to have a happy life. At first, I tried to talk myself out of doing it then. After all, it was the busy season at work and life as a whole wasn't bad. I was happy spending time at work—and with Brad—which was the majority of my time, and what was left over was time at home with Jessie.

As things had been falling apart, Jessie was spending more evenings out with his drinking buddies and as the daylight was lasting longer, I would go out with my best friends Sunshine and Lady for mind-clearing conversations and rides off into the sunset. I always trusted Sunshine and Lady and I understood my conversations with them better than I did with almost all human beings. It was very clear to me that they kept telling me that time was precious. There was never going to be a "good" time, so why waste more of my precious time? I planned to have my talk with Jessie the upcoming weekend.

When the weekend came, I continued to find reasons to put off the talk. On Sunday we were supposed to go over to Jessie's family for the first cookout of the year. That was my excuse for that day until it rained, and the cookout was called off. Jessie and I were going to be home for the whole day without any plans. The universe was speaking very clearly to me. Then, I guess the universe got tired of waiting for me, so it took matters into its own hands (spirit, energy, or whatever the universe uses). I was walking into the living room after starting the laundry and Jessie stopped me and asked, "Can we talk?"

I froze. This wasn't supposed to happen. This wasn't the plan. What was going on? I replied, "Sure."

He looked serious and very anxious. He spoke very quietly. "What's wrong? What has happened to us?"

I hadn't seen this coming at all. After being with Jessie for years, that was probably the deepest conversation we had ever had, and it was only two sentences. I sat there silently and Jessie continued to talk. Brad had told me a trick to get people to talk is to create an uncomfortable silence. People will talk to fill the void and usually say more than they want. It worked, but I have to admit that I wasn't doing it intentionally. I just didn't know what to say. Jessie had a lot to say with just a few words though. He told me that he knew things hadn't been good for a long time and that he had spent a lot of time trying to figure out what he had done to make things this way. He admitted he was not very good at these kinds of conversations, but he was desperate—desperate enough to force himself to talk to me in an attempt to work things out.

He was starting to tear up and his voice began to tremble. "I'm sorry for whatever I did. Just tell me what I need to do to fix it." He put his head down and sat there looking at the floor. I didn't know how to respond. I sat there, quiet. I hurt, not for me, but for him. I was sad, not for me, but for him. The only word that was going through my head was "truth." Up until then the search for truth was for me. The thought about Jessie's search for truth never crossed my mind. He had a truth, too, and was trying to figure it out and I didn't know what to tell him.

We both sat there in silence until the bell on the washing machine went off. I quietly said, "I have to get the laundry," and got up and walked away. When I came back to the living room, he was gone. I looked around the house, but he wasn't there. I had no idea where he'd gone but I was scared. Was he going to do something harmful to himself? Was he going to go out and get blasted with his friends? Whatever happened was going to be my fault. I had no inkling of what I should do. I decided to get in my truck and drive around to look for him. I didn't know what I would say if I found him but at least I would know he was alive. I couldn't find him anywhere. I decided to go and ask my best friends what to do next.

As I got closer to the horse barn, I saw Jessie's truck there. Why was Jessie at the horse barn? Was he going to do something to Sunshine and Lady? Was he going to hurt them to get back at me? I was in a panic and I jumped out of my truck and ran into the barn. Once again, I was stunned by what I saw. Jessie was sitting on a bale of hay having his own conversation with Sunshine and Lady. He turned to me, "If you can't tell me anything, I thought maybe they could."

I think it was the first time I'd ever felt Jessie's heart. I was confused about everything that was happening, internally and externally. I walked up to the stall and started to stroke Sunshine on her nose. I was facing away from Jessie, but was looking into Sunshine's eyes. The thought in my head about truth now changed to the other half of the equation: time was precious. I knew my feelings about Jessie were true to me and I knew they weren't going to change. That meant I would be wasting my, and his, precious time if I did nothing. It was clear to me that that was the time, the moment to move on. That is what got me through what happened next.

I didn't know what to say or how to start the conversation. My previously prepared speech was now obsolete; the perspective had changed. So, I just opened my mouth and said, "Jessie, this isn't about you, it's about me."

From there, the words came fluidly even though I had no idea what was coming next. "I have changed. I see and feel the world differently now. I understand things that I never did before. This new understanding is driving me to learn and understand more about life and myself. I can't really explain it all, but it is a great feeling and for the first time in my life I have a true passion to live for something. I'm not sure what that something is, but I know it's not you. I'm sorry that I haven't said anything to you until now, but I didn't know what this was all about. I was trying to blame you but I now know that this isn't about you. You haven't done anything wrong. We are just in different places."

Jessie broke in at that time, "Is this about the guy at the store?"

I wasn't expecting that question but now I had to come up with an answer and I wasn't sure what the truth was or what to tell him. What came out without any pre-thought was, "No. We have a friendship and we have good conversations, but it isn't about another man." I felt confused about what I had just said. I wasn't sure that was really the truth. I wasn't even sure if that was an answer to the question that Jessie had asked. It didn't seem to matter, though.

The look on Jessie's face was one of defeat. I think somehow the answer I gave him was clear to him or maybe he came to the realization that it was just over. There was nothing for him to fight for. He just sat there for a moment and then got up and walked over to me, "I just want you to be happy. I will go and stay at my parents' house until I can work out the details of moving out." The moment was over and the time to move on had arrived. I thought that I should feel sad or something that my marriage was over or that I had just shattered Jessie's life, but I didn't. I was excited that I now had a chance to move forward in my search for happiness. But it was the first time in a long time that I felt bad for Jessie. I didn't have any bad thoughts about him; he had tried to do the right thing through all of this but it didn't change anything for me.

By the end of the following week, Jessie had moved all of his things out of the house. All that was left was a note telling me he had everything and was moving in with one of his friends in case I needed to talk to him. There was no hint of bitterness or anger. He ended his note by saying that he had no regrets and that he loved me very much. He only wished the best for me. For a quick moment, I felt cheated that he was taking it so well, but then the thought turned into a peace that the smooth transition was a sign that this was the right thing—a confirmation of a new journey.

Chapter 17

THE FIRST STEP IN MY NEW REALITY WAS TELLING MY family what was going on and why I was leaving Jessie. My mother had a sense that I wasn't happy, but didn't say too much. Once in a while, she would fish for some details, but I didn't take the bait. My father, on the other hand, liked Jessie. He was old-fashioned about marriage, family, and having a grandson. I told myself that I had no idea how he was going to react, but that was just a lie. I knew damn well how he was going to react; I just didn't know how I was going to explain myself.

The next step was going to be much more intriguing: telling Brad. Jessie was not a topic we talked about much. I would go back and forth between feeling excited about sharing the news with Brad and feeling like I was telling Brad the way was clear for us to run off into the sunset together. After all, I had just thrown him a birthday party with a big surprise present. What other reason could there be for me leaving Jessie? I also wondered why I was even thinking about this in the first place! Was I turning into a giddy, boy-crazed teenage girl? I decided to put telling Brad about all of this on the back burner. After all, it was a subject we didn't talk about much anyway, so there was really no need to rush into it. But I couldn't say the same about telling my family.

It was an easy decision to tell my mom first. She wouldn't be happy about it, but I would probably still be alive after telling her. My father was not very good at paying attention to everything that was going on around him or reading between the lines. My mom, on the other hand, was very good at it. She and I did not have that "special" mother-daughter relationship; my father had the dibs on the special-relationship thing. Mom and I got along well and everything, but we didn't connect on that deeper level. Now I see that was more about me than her. She had been there waiting for me, but I hadn't been ready for that before. Now, I was. I needed someone to back me up and she was my only choice. I had no idea how I was going to start this dialogue. I started thinking about a conversation I'd had with Brad. He told me once that answers to our questions were all around us, but we didn't take time to listen to them. I decided to try it out and see if it was true. I had been doing much better with the trusting-my-gut thing and it seemed to be working, so why not on this?

I started to think about how things were surprisingly normal between Brad and me after the kiss. Our conversations were going well and we both seemed comfortable with each other. The store was getting busier with the spring season, but we were still finding time to talk. One day, I asked him how he found the courage to quit his secure day job to become a writer. I was amazed when he was able to answer quickly and precisely.

He said the "truth" was that he hated his day job and that "time is too precious to waste." Then he said that he came across a saying that sealed the deal. It said, "The fears of the present are the stepping stones to the future." I heard my answer. He was right; we just needed to listen better. I had the truth part, the precious time part, and now I understood the courage part. Talking with my mom was that first step.

My mom was the prototypical housewife. She took care of my dad and me and a majority of the household chores. She didn't express her opinions much, nor did my father seek her opinions. When she did share her thoughts, they were almost never challenged by me or my father. She had a part-time job that was full time in the summer. She would help me out in the store sometimes, especially in the spring while I was getting things ready for summer. She knew Brad from being at the store sometimes when he stopped by. I don't think she thought twice about anything more than him being just another customer. It was on one of those days she was helping me out at the store that the perfect opportunity for us to talk presented itself. I was kind of puzzled because it felt like the right time, but I was anxious about it. How could that be?

It was just the two of us in the store and we were rearranging some shelves when she straight out asked me how things were between Jessie and me. She wasn't just fishing this time. I said that things were fine. Technically they were, but that wasn't the point. Then—completely out of character—she said, "Really, Mack?" My mom had called me Mack. She never called me Mack. I was always Mackenzie to her because I was a girl whether my father liked it or not. That was just her way of giving a passive reaction to my father.

My mom then pulled the silent treatment on me—you know, the one that Brad told me about where people talk to avoid awkward silence. It really does work. I couldn't stop talking. I told her everything that had happened with Jessie. I was able to refrain from saying a word about Brad, though. She didn't react at all. She was very calm and just let me keep talking.

When I was finally out of words she said, "I am your mother, Mack, and I want you to know that you can trust me and I will support you. I want you to be happy." I heard it! She said she would support me! Step One Courage: Mom. Check. But just like the game shows where the next level always gets more difficult, so would talking with my father.

My biggest fear was that I thought my father would think I was a failure for not making my marriage work, that I wasn't trying hard enough. I just knew he was going to side with Jessie, the head of the household who worked to provide me with a good life. I knew he would not understand all of this "feeling" stuff. I knew that the special bond I had with my father was going to be over, and I couldn't deal with that. It didn't matter though, because I was already committed to what was happening and my mom already knew. Mom invited me over for dinner one night and of course, Jessie was not going to be there with me. I was going to have to explain why and I couldn't lie to my dad. But it turned out I didn't have to, because he never asked about Jessie.

After dinner, Dad took his normal place in his chair in the living room while I was helping Mom pick up the dishes. Mom just said, "It's time. Go talk to your dad. It will be okay." It was like Mom had hypnotized me. I walked into the living room kind of numb, but without fear.

Dad just looked at me and said, "How's my little girl?"

I started to cry. "Did Mom talk to you?"

"She just said to talk with you." Then it got scary. He started to talk with me as if he knew exactly what I was afraid of. After he spent what seemed like an hour telling me everything was going to be alright and how much he loved me, he asked me if all of this was about Jessie.

What? He had no idea what happened. His whole talk was just a prelude to the issue. But I was okay. I told him the whole story just like I'd told Mom. He told me it was okay. Sometimes people just weren't meant to be together. All he wanted was for me to be happy and he asked if there was anything he could do to help. I said he'd already done everything I needed. I gave him the biggest hug I had ever given. Again, by following my heart, I realized that my truth was so rewarding when I had the courage to have faith and act. Courage Step Two: Dad. Check.

I felt energized, free, and determined that I was on my way. My life was becoming exciting and full of passion. I was really figuring out everything I had been missing while I had just been showing up for life. I just wanted to keep going and learning more, experiencing more. But there was still another step I needed to take: telling Brad what was going on. I decided to take a break and just enjoy my moment and worry about that later. I went back to my store the next day, but it felt like I was stepping into a whole new world. Everything around me was the same but everything inside of me was brand new. I just needed to learn how to use all the new understanding I had discovered.

Chapter 18

AFTER JESSIE AND I SEPARATED, I STARTED EXPERI-
encing a new type of personal freedom. Up until then, my
whole life had been attached to something: my parents, school,
Jessie, or my business. Now, I was done with school, lived on
my own, Jessie was gone, and I was in control of the store. I realized that in the past I was afraid of freedom. I was afraid to be
responsible for my own decisions and my own life. Now, I was
ready to embrace that freedom. I was gaining an understanding
of the world, the spirit around me. This newfound discovery
was giving me the tools I needed to navigate my own direction
and that was exhilarating to me. However, there was still one
thing I was attached to: Brad. But there was a big difference
because I wasn't clinging to something, I was being drawn by
something. I want to say I was being drawn by the opportunity
to be something I never thought I could be. The truth was,
though, that I couldn't say that I wasn't drawn to the man.

As it got closer to summer, business was picking up and
Brad was an active participant at the store. When I asked many

of the new customers coming in how they'd heard about the store they would tell me about something I'd had no part in doing. I began to figure out that Brad was putting his retail experience to use and not telling me. He was giving all the credit to me and then telling me how proud he was of me. That just attracted me to him even more.

Our conversations continued to be more fluent. It never felt like we were having deep talks, but looking back, they were more intimate than I thought. I'd never had these kinds of talks with anyone, except Sunshine and Lady. He was asking more questions about my past and my life experiences. I never felt I had any interesting experiences to talk about, but he would keep telling me that every person had a story to tell. I would think, *Yeah, maybe, but that doesn't mean they're good stories.* I was more interested in hearing his stories. I wanted to know how he got so smart about life. I was becoming more and more absorbed in his life and the wealth of knowledge and wisdom he possessed. I wanted to learn it all from him.

Oddly, I was also becoming more frustrated at how well the store was doing. We would begin talking about something so fascinating and then have to suspend the conversation because of the damn customers! Eventually, this led to coming in a little earlier and staying a bit after work. After all, I didn't have to get home and cook dinner for Jessie. Strangely, Brad never asked me about that.

I wasn't missing my wifely responsibilities. I wasn't missing Jessie, either. I wasn't sure how Jessie was doing since our separation, but he wasn't intruding on my life so I didn't think much about it. I'd heard from him a few times since, but there was never any drama about it. We didn't talk about divorce or what was next for us. In contrast, he even filled in for me at the store one time when I wanted to go to a horse show out of town for a couple of days. That was more than he'd ever done for me when we were together. I thought about asking Brad to fill in for me, but then I would have to do some explaining to my family. I wasn't ready for that and I wasn't sure if I ever would be. Things were going fine just the way they were and I didn't want to disrupt those things. I did know that someday I would have to address all of this with my family and Brad—just not today, tomorrow, or in the foreseeable future.

With everything that had been happening in the past couple of months—with Jessie and me, my parents and me, the store doing well, and Brad and I getting closer—I was feeling pretty good about myself. I felt like I was a totally different person with a totally different perspective about everything. I didn't know whether it was growing up and gaining maturity and wisdom, or just observation. I liked the direction things were heading and I wanted to keep going down that road, but at a much faster speed. But thanks to my newfound wisdom, I realized I didn't want to get reckless about my trip. I needed a road map to get where I was going and that road map was Brad.

Brad was smart, worldly, articulate, and married. I was attracted to all of that except the being married part. There was nothing adulterous about our relationship. The kiss was a present, and nothing else like that had happened since, so technically we were still just friends. Did Brad feel the same? Did Emily feel the same? Did she even know about me? Whenever those questions came to mind, I had to dismiss them immediately. If I asked those questions, then I would have to look for those answers. Those answers might not coincide with my accepted perception that we were just friends. There were increasingly more moments of me wondering about Emily. Who was she and what did Brad see in her? Of course, I did not like her because she must have been a horrible cheating wife forcing Brad to look for love elsewhere and to be with me. What a bitch! There was no way a sweet and sincere man like Brad would spend time with another woman—me—if he was being treated properly. She must really be a bitch!

But I knew better than that because Brad would tell me so. He always spoke very lovingly about Emily and how she understood him and trusted him. He didn't talk about her much, but when he did it was clear how he felt about her. For me it was just easier to think of her as a bitch. Besides, if she wasn't a bitch wouldn't that make me the bitch? I'd kissed him . . . Oh, wait. I almost forgot; that was a present. Let's just move on.

I tried to avoid talking to Brad about his present-day life. I would usually ask him about "his story" and focus on his past and how he'd learned to navigate his life so well. That was what I wanted to learn about anyway. There was one day I was thinking about how much time he was spending at the store with me and wondering if he was getting any writing done. Wouldn't Emily be asking about that? Brad never really spoke to me about his writing. On the few occasions I did ask what he was writing about he would simply say, "Life." How does a person make a career or living writing just about life? I guess when you really think about, it isn't everything about "life"?

Then I thought, wouldn't it be really neat, and convenient for me, if he was writing a book about all of his philosophies—you know, a kind of how-to book for finding peace? I told him that once and he just looked at me with a slight smile and shook his head. "That would be just my story. Everybody has their own story." I felt like he was trying to tell me something, but I never could figure out what.

One time I asked in passing, "Have you written anything lately?"

He looked directly at me and said, "I am always writing—it just doesn't always make it from my head to the paper." I knew how true that was because there were so many times I would look over at him and I could see his mind working and I could feel some sort of deep energy coming from him. I just didn't know what to call it.

Brad had a lot of stories from his past to tell. That was one reason I felt my stories were inadequate; I didn't have all those years to draw from. I could never say that to him though, because he tended to be a bit sensitive about his age. I noticed that he did not have many stories from the recent past; they all seemed to be from many years ago. Another thing I picked up on was a kind of theme that ran through his stories. He would speak of this trip to Colorado as a teenager with such joy and excitement. He talked about it being life-changing, unforgettable, and so impactful on his life. He told me the name he had for it: his "vision quest." He told me how it had become a regular event each year and how it always taught him something. He said it kept his life on course.

As our conversations continued to progress, I started to refer to his vision quests, seeking some additional details. I was becoming more intrigued with each story he told me about these quests. Why didn't I have something like that? How do you get something like that? I wanted to know. I tried not to press too hard for details because these journeys were very personal to him and he was very protective about some of his stories. He would refer to them as "his stories," and I was amazed each time he shared one of his experiences. I desperately wanted some of my own stories. I got it now.

In our daily conversations we covered any and all subjects and topics. It didn't matter what the subject or topic was—he always had a story with an appropriate lesson to go with it. It wasn't a know-it-all type of story, but one that would make sense and bring a smile to his face and mine. I think he became frustrated at times because I never wanted to talk about myself. I didn't feel like I had anything interesting to say, and besides, I was trying to soak up all he had to offer.

I noticed that Emily was never part of any of these stories and I decided to break our unwritten rule about talking about our spouses and ask him about her. He didn't seem hesitant to talk about her. He actually was very matter-of-fact about it. He said that when Emily and he first got together the vision quest was kind of a romantic adventure and getaway for them. That lasted for several years but Emily really wasn't the camping kind of girl. (Oh yeah! I had something on Emily!) It eventually turned into their independent vacations. It was something they were both happy about and he said it worked well for them.

I asked Brad what made these trips so special to him. He got a smile on his face and his whole body just seemed to relax. Even the tone of his voice was soft and content. "Everything about it is special. Being outdoors, the peace and quiet and all the time to just sit and think."

"Think about what?"

Of course, his response was, "About life." Then, to my surprise, he continued to talk. "I would think about all of the questions I had about everything. Then I would wait for a shooting star and make a wish for all of the answers."

I started to laugh. I thought he was joking, but when I noticed the look on his face, I knew he wasn't. I couldn't remember anytime that I'd been with Brad when I felt he was upset with me, until that moment. He got very quiet and suddenly that smile on his face, the relaxed body language, and the soft tone of his voice all disappeared. I didn't know what had happened, but I was scared. Whatever it was had to have been my fault. I had no idea how to fix it either.

Then Brad began to talk again. "When I was around eight years old, I would go out on our back porch and lay on the ground looking at the stars for hours. Some nights it would be quite late, but my mom would let me stay up because she knew how much I enjoyed it. I really can't say why I enjoyed it so much back then. Even now. I would do this every opportunity that I could. Then life took over. Before I knew it there were girls, work, and I was in my tweens, then high school."

I wanted to bust out laughing again but not after what had just happened. He paused for dramatic effect then looked at me. Then he broke into laughter. He jumped back into his story. "It wasn't until I was out of high school and took my trip to Colorado that I rediscovered that feeling. I felt like I had hooked up with an old friend." Even though the story had a childlike fairy tale feel to it, I was hooked on every word and waiting to hear the moral of the story. Brad went on, "It felt like the universe was talking to me through the shooting stars. I would talk back, asking my questions.

"I had a teacher in high school who gave us an assignment to journal for a whole month. I'm still journaling today. These stargazing trips became the impetus to my journal and the journal became the workbook to my life." I now understood why he'd become upset when I'd laughed; I had reduced his heart and soul to child's play. I never looked at fairy tales and children's stories the same way ever again.

I learned a big lesson from that experience. Life was complex, but the answers didn't have to be. I had been watching Brad impressively navigate life with a simplistic yet powerful approach. He made me see that peace and happiness could be achieved and he had the knowledge to do it. I wanted that knowledge. I just wasn't sure how I was going to get it. I gained a lot of insight from that conversation, which then became the foundation of understanding Brad. That was another new perspective I had never experienced before. There was never a calculated approach to using that insight in any future conversations, but it seemed to shine a light on the direction of our journey.

It had been more than a year since I first met Brad, but it felt like I had known him my entire life. I couldn't imagine my life without him. I also could not imagine my life with him.

I was becoming increasingly more confused about the feelings that I had for him. He was part father, part best friend, and—even bigger—part school-girl crush. There had been a lot of things that happened but there was much more that needed to happen. Jessie and I needed to come to some kind of closure about our marriage. I needed to come to some kind of terms with my feelings for Brad. Then I needed to somehow get my family to come to some kind of terms with Brad. I tried to convince myself that summer was here and there just wasn't going to be any time to deal with these big issues so they would just have to wait. Life was going well, and I was confident I was in control. I should have been smart enough at this stage of my development to know that you don't tell the universe when to do things. It didn't work that way. Unfortunately, I had to find that out the hard way.

Chapter 19

I'D BEEN LOOKING FORWARD TO SUMMER. EVEN though it was very busy at the store, there was still plenty of time to play. Longer days meant more time with Sunshine and Lady and just hanging out at the park or going swimming. I loved the warmer weather because I didn't have to wear gloves, hats, and big bulky coats. I didn't know if this was an actual fact but it always seemed like good things tended to happen in the summer. Things were already going well, so I had really high expectations for that summer. My thoughts were running wild with what some of those good things were going to be and if Brad was going to be a part of them. We were heading into June with the temperatures heating up; I kept wondering just how hot it would get.

I was not one of those girls who thought about every outfit they put on to make sure the pants were tight enough and the neckline low enough. My criteria centered on whether it was warm enough in the winter and cool enough in the summer. I never spent much money on my clothes because they didn't matter to me; they were going to get very dirty and torn very quickly. That part was the boy in me. But like everything else in my life, that was changing too.

I'd always liked wearing short-shorts and tank tops in the summer. I didn't like being sweaty in my clothes. It used to drive my dad crazy because my shorts were always too short and my tops were always too revealing. I never understood that, but my dad insisted that all men were sexual predators and I was their prey. I would just laugh. My dad never pushed it because he knew I could take care of myself. Jessie was even more critical of my wardrobe choices and was not shy about letting me know how he felt about it. He didn't push it too far though, because I think he liked showing me off to his friends. But now, I was suddenly thinking about what I was going to wear every day. I was concerned that I was tanning evenly and I wasn't sweating like a pig. I also found myself not liking being called Mack anymore; I wanted to be Mackenzie. Brad usually did call me Mackenzie and would only use Mack for special effect. That was okay.

The only thing Brad would say about how I dressed was that I always looked good no matter what I was wearing. Brad was someone who I never heard make any inappropriate comments about women and I never saw him gawking at them or slobbering with his tongue sticking out. Once in a while I would catch him sneaking a glance at me. I never thought it was creepy; in fact, I thought it was very flattering and I liked it. I didn't think anybody had noticed that there was something going on between Brad and me. I hadn't said anything to anyone about us and when we were together there wasn't anything obvious to make people notice. I chose not to say anything to anybody because the truth of the matter was, I didn't know what to tell them. I didn't know what to even call whatever it was we were. I didn't think Brad had told anybody about our relationship either.

I wasn't sure what he was telling Emily. She had to be wondering something, didn't she? Although I tried to avoid thinking about the relationship between Brad and Emily, I couldn't help but wonder what it was like. I couldn't imagine any problems, but what wife would allow her husband so much time away from home without an explanation? I was having a hard time when Brad left me to go home to Emily. Could Brad be like every other guy everyone talks about? The smooth operator, the player? My gut was very clear that he wasn't, and I had been starting to trust my gut more and more. The fact of the matter was that even though I didn't like to see him go home, I still trusted him. I could only see him from the point of how he treated me. At least that was how I justified it to myself.

Going back to what I said about there not having been any more physical engagement since the birthday surprise, I'm not really sure that was totally true. With the daily lunches at the picnic table and moving stuff around and handing things off to each other, there were increasing moments of incidental contacts. I'm not sure the word "incidental" was totally accurate either. Maybe it had always just happened but I was certainly noticing it more—and feeling it more. And I admit it made me feel good and I liked it. I only wished that I knew what was going on in Brad's head. Was he thinking the same things I was? If he was, he sure wasn't showing it. Maybe I was just hallucinating about all of this or maybe Brad was gay. Maybe he was just a good guy who did not want to cross any lines. It seemed like I was giving Brad a lot of opportunities, and permission, to have his way with me but he never went there. Was there something wrong with me? Was I not pretty enough or sexy enough? What else could I do? I certainly did not plan for what happened next.

I hadn't been to see Sunshine and Lady in a while, so I decided to pay them a visit after work one night. It had been some time since I had saddled up and gone for a ride. It would be some time before I would be able to saddle up again. I guess I was out of form and I fell off Sunshine. The fall really banged up my leg but fortunately I didn't break it. But I'd have to stay off of it for a couple of weeks and it was not a good time for that to happen. It was the busiest time of the year at the store and my mom was working full time during the summer at her job and I wasn't going to ask Jessie for help. I only had one idea about what I could do that would work best—ask Brad. He was there most of the time anyway, and he knew how to run things. He was actually better at running the store than I was.

Just as I was about to text Brad and explain what had happened, I got a text from him. He asked me if I was okay. Huh? How did he know? He said he'd been to the store and my mom told him what had happened. He wasn't surprised because he knew I had a history of being accident-prone. He was more than willing to help out and actually seemed quite excited about it. I knew I could get through this with Brad's help but then I'd have to explain to everybody who Brad really was to me. I knew that wouldn't go well. Then I was reminded of my horoscope from the past: "Do not put things off because time is precious, but know that truth is more precious than time." It reminded me that I should not tell the universe when I wanted to do things. Instead, it was the universe telling me that it was time for me to tell the truth.

Chapter 20

THERE WASN'T GOING TO BE MUCH TIME TO COME UP with a solution to my problem. I decided to go back to the plan that had worked for me before: talk to Mom first. Since I'd gone to Mom about what was going on with Jessie, we had become closer. It still wasn't that deep mother-daughter bond, but it was going in a good direction. I prayed that it would keep going in that direction. I wasn't as nervous about this talk as I'd been the last time because of how well that one went. Since Mom kind of knew who Brad was, I took the approach that telling her he was a good regular customer who'd "retired" from retail management and would be the ideal option to get through this situation. I was very confident that my plan was perfect, and that Mom wouldn't be a problem. After I gave her my pitch, she was very calm. She asked me some simple basic questions without bias or judgment. She asked me if I had concerns. I said that I was good with this plan and she said okay. But then, she then asked me if I was comfortable with this man and asked if I trusted him.

Suddenly, these questions didn't seem like they were about the issue at hand. It wasn't what she said, but it was what my gut was telling me. I sensed that she sensed there was more to this story. But then she said that if I could convince my father she'd be okay with it. I wondered if she was okay with it because she thought there was no way in hell my father would agree to this.

I waited until Friday night to get in the ring with dad. I was prepared to go the distance. It didn't matter because it was a knockout in the first round. I didn't have a chance. He exploded and yelled at me like he had never done before. There was no, "You're my little girl and I will love and support you with anything." It was completely opposite from my interaction with him about me leaving Jessie. I guess I was no longer on his pedestal. He wouldn't listen to one word I had to say. I didn't even get the chance to fully make my pitch. He just went into this angry tirade. When he finished yelling, the "talk" was over and he stormed out of the room.

I was devastated. I'd known my father would be against this, but I hadn't thought he would react like that. I felt disowned and abandoned by the man who'd given me everything. I ran through the pain in my leg, crying. I didn't even go into the barn to be with Sunshine and Lady; I didn't want them to see me like this. I stayed outside all night staring up at the stars. I really wanted to be that far away. Then, I saw a shooting star.

I was in no mood to be awed, but I did make a wish. I yelled, "I just want to live my life!" I felt an emptiness inside as vast as the universe. I finally stopped crying and just sat there for a while. The talk with Brad about shooting stars popped into my head. It calmed me and I was able to pull myself back together and realign my thinking. An energy started welling up inside me and it kept building until it hit me: what was the truth here? The truth was I wanted to be with Brad, and this was my store and it should be my decision. I was a grown woman now and I could make my own decisions and I was done being told what to do. I just sat there in a kind of trance for the rest of the night.

Then I watched the sunrise. I have seen a lot of sunrises working on a farm, but I never really watched one like I was watching this one: it was different, I was different. It was telling me that this was a new day. I don't remember how long it was before my dad came out to take care of the horses. He didn't realize I was there but when he did, he just stopped. He looked at me with a glare and stated, "I'm done talking."

That was the bell to start the rematch. A side of me came out that I didn't even know existed and neither did my father. I wasn't even thinking about what I was saying but the words just came pouring out with a very defined purpose. My father had no choice but to listen. His glare turned into tears. I paused for a second, fearing I wouldn't be able to continue. My father stood there with no words to say. I went on for a few more words about love and trust. Then, I left. I don't remember where I went or for how long, but I came back a different person. I was my own person now.

It was later that afternoon when my father drove up, got out of his truck and began walking up to the door. My gut told me to settle down and be calm. This was difficult after everything that had happened. My father came to the door and asked if he could say a few things.

"Go ahead."

He told me how sorry he was and how I had been right about everything I'd said. Then he said, "I'm proud of you, Mackenzie."

It was the hardest thing I'd ever had to do, but I was able to hold back my tears. I still had more to say. I asked him, "Why did you get so upset? You don't even know Brad and you didn't even consider my thoughts. Don't you trust me?"

"It's not that. I trust you completely."

"Then what is it?"

"I've been watching you grow up right in front of my eyes from a little cowgirl to a woman. I feel like you don't need me anymore. You're moving on with your life and you're able to take care of yourself. I'm out of a job." He cried, "Please forgive me for acting the way I did."

This time I couldn't hold back my tears. "Dad, I will always need you. You are my rock and always will be."

He cleared his throat and quietly asked, "Why didn't you ask me to help out at the store?"

Oh, I am such a dumbass! I hadn't even thought of that option! This wasn't about Brad at all; it was about me replacing Dad with Brad. My dad did trust me. I didn't know how I could have been so stupid and not seen what was really happening. I told him that I hadn't asked him to help out at the store because he had his fishing trip scheduled and, besides, I didn't think he could handle me being his boss. We both laughed and gave each other a big hug.

While I was hugging him, he whispered in my ear, "Do you want to go feed the ducks at the park?" That was something we used to do when I was a little girl and right now, I just wanted to be his little girl again.

"Yes."

At the pond, we probably had the best talk we'd ever had. He asked me a lot of questions about life. Real questions. And I gave him real answers. We talked about Brad in the way girls talk about their boyfriends with their dads.

He said that Brad sounded like a great guy and I responded, "But he is not my father." I thought about those words more later. They felt like I was trying to tell myself something. I had eluded at times about Brad being a father-like figure in my life, but it was now apparent to me that he wasn't my father. That relationship was something totally different. The type of role that Brad played in my life was really, really starting to narrow down. That was starting to excite me and scare me at the same time. After Dad dropped me off at home, I immediately sent a text to Brad telling him to be at the shop Monday morning and *Don't be late!* He had a job to do and I was going to be his new boss. This was a role I was really looking forward to.

Chapter 21

IT HAD ALMOST BEEN A WHOLE WEEK SINCE I'D LAST seen Brad. We had sent some texts back and forth a few times but with all the chaos the texts were not very long or informative of all the activity going on. I was feeling like my whole life had taken another step in a new direction, because it had. I no longer had a husband and the relationship with my family was on a completely different level. It was a lot to happen in just a few weeks' time. Now my thoughts were turning to how this was all going to affect my relationship with Brad. I was now going to be his boss and he was going to be caring for me. We would be spending a significant amount of time together.

I also had a lot to tell him about everything that had been going on and I wasn't sure just how I was going to do that or when I—I mean the universe—was going to be ready to do it. I was a liberated woman now and I wondered how that would change anything between Brad and me. This was also no longer a secret with my family. They still didn't understand the complete scope of our relationship, but Brad was now part of my unfolding story. After the course of negotiations about Brad helping out at the store and my parents jumping on board with that, they even suggested that they would like to meet him. I hadn't been expecting that twist in my plot. My mom had met Brad a couple of times at the store and from what my mom could remember she thought he was very nice. I was going with that. It seemed a little weird because they were kind of treating him like he was a new boyfriend but they knew he was married. I guess I couldn't blame them because they probably picked up some parental vibe that something was going on. At least that was what my paranoia was telling me.

When I got to the store Monday morning Brad was already there. I was impressed because it was always a good sign for an employee to show up early for their first day on the job. I was excited about seeing him again and he seemed excited to see me again, too. He jumped out of his car and walked over toward me and stood there with a big smile. I opened the door and yelled at him to help his disabled boss out of her truck. I was joking when I said this because even in my physical state, I was totally capable of getting into the store myself. The more I thought about it, I started realizing this could really be a lot of fun. I was already liking this boss thing. He came over to the truck and put his arm around my back and under my legs and picked me up and then carried me into the store. I joked about breaking his back and having a worker's comp claim on his first day. I could feel him gently squeeze me a little bit harder. When he set me down, we both hung on to each other for what was definitely longer than necessary, but neither of us seemed eager to let go. My new life was feeling good right then and I was already convinced I was going to be a fun boss.

I was impressed at how seriously he was taking his new role as my subordinate. He did the job extraordinarily well. I hated to say it, but he did it better than I did. I was even more impressed at how well he was taking care of me. He was taking such good care of me that it was slowing down my healing process and I wasn't sure when I would be able to return back to full duty. It could be a while. We were having a lot of fun. Our conversations seemed to be on the light side. We talked about everything—high school and dating and all those embarrassing moments that left us in tears. But I wasn't finding any good time to talk about the evolving circle of life that I was going through. No hurry.

There was one particular conversation that caught my attention. I asked him if he would have asked me out if we had been in high school together. It surprised me when he said no without even thinking about it. I wasn't quite sure how to take that. We were being silly at the time but there was no follow-up to say, "I'm just kidding." Not even after a whole minute! That hurt! It did get me thinking though about how it would be for us to date each other—not just then but what about now? As the conversation continued my hurt turned into intrigue. He said if he had met me in high school, he would have been too chicken to talk to me, let alone ask me out because I was so cute. Aww. I was okay with that.

But what about now? That was what I really wanted to know, but I couldn't ask him, could I? The conversation turned to what our ideas of the perfect date was. He told me his thoughts about what was not the perfect date, but he would not elaborate on what he thought would be the perfect date. In return, he asked me about what I would have done if he had asked me out in high school.

Sticking with the tone of the discussion, I responded very coyly and said, "Some things need to be left a mystery to the universe." I thought it was a good tease when I said it but later, I regretted my comment. What if saying that affirmed his belief that a girl like me was a snob and would never have gone out with him? That wasn't what I wanted him to think. At that point, I redirected the conversation. I told him that my perfect date was all the things that he said were not his perfect date. I intended my comments to be said sarcastically, indicating that I was making fun of the same things, but again I thought that I may have made him feel inferior to my status and that I would have never gone out with him. I decided I wasn't doing very well with this line of conversation, so I thought it would be best to totally change direction before I dug myself into a deeper hole that I couldn't get out of.

Overall, our conversations remained light and less serious. That was giving me a false sense that we didn't need to go down the road of full disclosure yet. Slowly, more in-depth moments started to find their way into our dialogue. With my limited activity I was forced into spending an unbearable amount of time sitting around and doing nothing. That was something I didn't think I had ever done before; it wasn't in my DNA. I was a high-energy person, the person who was always on the move. The moment I stopped I would simply crash into a deep sleep to regain my energy and then return to action upon awakening. The only thing that was salvaging my inactivity was the attention Brad was giving me.

That extensive amount of downtime led me to start doing something Brad told me he did. He would make up stories about the people who came into the store. I found this to be quite entertaining and stimulating. It wasn't physically stimulating but it was mentally energizing. That was another new territory for me. Sharing these stories with Brad provided a whole new resource for topics that led to more questions for us to talk about—a kind of field laboratory. That new territory led me to a new dimension in my life where I was asking more questions and seeking answers to the meaning of life. I think Brad thought it was kind of funny. The talks were becoming longer and progressively deeper. The interruptions by the customers (how dare they!) were becoming increasingly frustrating because we could not finish our talks. The frustration became so significant that I finally asked him if he wanted to stay later after work to finish our conversations. Without even thinking about it he said, "Sure, sounds like fun."

I couldn't believe it when I thought about what I'd done and that I'd done it without even getting nervous. This act of courage hadn't been driven by my wanting to spend time with Brad, but was truly about our conversations. Although spending time with Brad was a nice benefit, too. We ordered a pizza and had a wonderful date—I mean working dinner. From then on, it wasn't unusual for us to stay late. It was summer and the store was busy, so sometimes overtime was mandatory. I was the boss and it was my call to make.

The responses Brad gave me about my questions all made a lot of sense to me. This allowed me to relax and not think so much about whether I was asking stupid and ridiculous questions. Instead, I was becoming engaged and eager to learn and understand even more. The more I learned, the less I understood; the less I understood, the more I wanted to learn. I was like the little kid who kept asking their parent, *Why? Why? Why?* I'm sure I was driving Brad crazy just like kids do, but I didn't care; I was growing. All this new perspective was carrying over into my daily life. I was no longer just creating stories about people but now I was also watching how Brad was interacting with everyone and everything. He was always so calm and patient. He always seemed so happy and content. I realized I'd never known Brad to want for anything, at least not like everyone else. He never talked about the fancy car or extravagant lifestyle that everyone else dreams about. As a matter of fact, he never talked about anything he wanted but he was always asking everybody else what they wanted, especially me. How could I not have seen this before? That is when I experienced my epiphany. What was it that I really wanted? The truth became very apparent to me: I wanted what Brad had. It was okay if he came with it, too.

I was so excited about my new discovery that I couldn't hold it back and had to tell somebody. So, I told Brad. He was the only person I knew who would understand what I was talking about and experiencing. There was no game-playing or posturing around the other dynamics surrounding our relationship. This was much more important. I can't even remember his first reaction to my sharing. I was like a little kid tasting chocolate for the first time. I told him that I wanted him to teach me everything he knew. I paused for a moment to wait for him to yell, "Hallelujah! You got it!" But that didn't happen.

Instead I got, "You want me to teach you what?"

How could he not be excited like I was? I started to panic, thinking, *Did I just do something really stupid?* I felt like crawling under a rock and crying. I was confused but I wasn't sure about what.

Then Brad asked me, "What is it that you want to learn?" For some reason, that calmed me down and brought back my excitement. I could sense his confusion and realized he wasn't judging me; he was seriously trying to understand me.

I explained the things I was observing about him that I wanted to learn for myself. Things like contentment, peace, and happiness. He sat there quietly, contemplating everything I was saying.

Finally, he looked right at me. "Thank you. I never realized I had accomplished what I was searching for until you just told me. Now I know wishes can come true."

That last statement puzzled me, but I would save my additional questions for another day. This day needed to be savored for our mutual but individual discoveries. We both left that day equally dazed and perplexed by all this new information we were processing about ourselves. I could tell he was thinking about where his life was supposed to be going from here, while I was thinking about going back to school. I had a lot to learn but I knew what I wanted to major in and who I wanted to be my teacher.

Chapter 22

THE NEXT TIME WE WERE TOGETHER, IT WAS A LITTLE different than usual. There was less of the awkward-boy-and-girl thing going on. Instead, it was a feeling of something much deeper and more intimate. I don't mean intimate as in physically or sexually, but emotionally. We didn't specifically talk about our previous conversation and epiphany, but it felt like it was understood and would be the building block for moving forward to the next chapter. It kind of felt like we were both waiting for someone to take the lead and tell us both what that next move should be. It seemed like we were trying to be normal, but our minds were preoccupied with deep, intense thought. That lasted for days and I wondered how being away from each other over the weekend would impact the place we were both in. The question was answered when the activities of the weekend took care of the next week's direction for conversation.

That Saturday night, my dad called out of the blue and invited me to go to church with them. That was quite a shock since we were not a church-going family. We used to go on special occasions like Christmas and Easter when I was little but we had not attended in many years. I didn't want to say yes, but I couldn't say no to my dad, especially after what we'd just gone through. I didn't even joke about what the special occasion was for the sudden trip to church or if he remembered how to get there. It all felt way too serious and I did not want to disrespect my father for whatever reason brought this on.

I don't know how to describe that Sunday. I felt very uneasy, and not because I hadn't been there in years and I was afraid of being struck by lightning. It was more like I was going to the high school prom—and I don't mean as a chaperone. My mom told me that it was Dad's idea; she didn't know why he wanted to go and she couldn't say no either. How do you tell someone you don't want to go to church with them? He was very serious about it, but in keeping with his character he didn't say anything about what made him suddenly want to go. After the service, he invited me over for a family day. We cooked out and spent the day talking to each other and just having a nice time. It had been quite a while since we had done anything like that. I had to admit that part of it made the trip to church bearable. The next day, I couldn't wait to tell Brad about my weekend.

That talk carried us through the whole week. I think we were both trying to keep that topic going so we didn't have to continue with the previous conversation or come up with a follow-up to that one. Going to church seemed like a topic that was out in the distance and we were both talking about it as though it were a neutral experience or as if it had happened to someone else. It kind of normalized things for us a bit. We got back to some lighthearted banter with a few laughs later in the week. We really needed that to take the edge off the intensity of talking about God. But I went right back to the God conversation on Friday when my mom called and asked me to go with them again on Sunday. I really hadn't thought this was going to be a regular thing and I did not want to go back that weekend or any time in the future. I saw God differently now and it wasn't in the church. I would always tell people that I believed in God, but I did not belong to any church. The truth was I hated going and after the previous weekend that hadn't changed. In fact, I think it had made it worse for me. I did believe in God, but I never really put any more thought into it past that.

I told Brad about my mom's invitation and he already knew how I was feeling about all of it. I asked him what he thought I should do. He asked me why I would want to go. I thought about it for a moment, "For my dad."

"Then go for your dad. That's your truth. You don't have to go for any other reason or justify your reasons for going to anybody. You do it for your own reasons." His answer was so simple, yet it felt so right. This was why I wanted to learn from Brad. He always made things simple yet very profound. I looked at this as my first lesson, but I wasn't going to tell Brad that. It would just freak him out and I didn't want to impede our progress.

I did go to church with my family and this time I was more prepared. I did not feel as agitated as I had the week before. Oddly enough, I spent the time listening and paying attention to everything; the words that were said, all the rituals, and the people in the pews. I was looking for something to make sense to me but the only thing that was making sense was that it wasn't making any sense. What I did notice was that all these people were looking for something. They were looking for their own truth, their own peace and happiness.

That stayed on my mind for the remainder of the day, but it wasn't creating any anxiety over not having an answer for everything. As a matter of fact, it made me feel like I was not the only person in search of something. Maybe I wasn't concerned about having any answers because I knew that when I talked with Brad about all of this, I would get my answers. I sent Brad a text and asked him if he could come in early so I could talk to him about my experience before the day got in our way.

He quickly responded, *Sure. I'm looking forward to the overtime pay.* I loved that Brad could always throw in a comment to make me laugh or at least smile. We continued to stay after the store closed almost every night, just to talk. This gave us a chance to have no pressure over time or the interference of those damn customers getting in the way. It was a regular part of our day and our relationship now. School was in session.

It seemed like a natural progression for us to start talking about all the lessons I wanted Brad to teach me again. He had initially been shocked and overcome with fear when I first asked him to be my mentor. Now, he took the opportunity of our new freedom to talk to bring up that topic to me first. He told me that he'd been thinking a lot about that conversation and that he didn't know what to do about it. He said he wasn't a priest or minister or even appropriately educated to teach such a complicated subject. He said that if he were to go down that road, he would feel like a cult leader recruiting a following for his own religion.

I laughed and told him not to think so highly of himself. Then I got serious. "I just want to hear your story. Let me learn from your story. That's a lesson you've already taught me." I could tell that I'd really stumped him with that and that he was at a loss for words and didn't know what to say.

Finally, he said he had no idea where to begin and that there were no books or course curriculum to follow. I said, "Start with your experience of when you first remember asking about life." He paused for a moment and then a slight smile came to his face. Then, he looked at me and the words finally started to come.

He started off, "It goes back to those nights on my back porch as a young kid I told you about. I found looking into the universe to be so mysterious yet calming. It always felt like the universe was trying to tell me the story of what my life was going to be. At that age, I had no reason not to believe what I was hearing. As far as I knew that's what everybody did. Periodically my mom would ask me what I was always thinking about and I would say—"

I interrupted, "What else? Life."

He laughed and said sarcastically, "Of course!" He continued, "Later on, my mom told me that she found it strange for something so deep to be coming out of the mouth of an eight-year-old boy, but what could she do? She just went with the flow because she couldn't see anything bad coming out of it. As I grew, life got busy and hectic, so my time with the stars dwindled. That is, until high school, when I met this older guy—by 'older,' I mean nineteen. We met in a junior bowling league and then later became friends through a guitar group at church. Looking back, that would probably be pretty questionable in a creepy way today. We both had a man-crush on John Denver and we became inspired by nature and the mountains and such."

I never knew Brad could play the guitar. That was something that I found kind of attractive in guys, but I really didn't know anything about John Denver. It was just one more thing that drew me to him.

Brad continued, "We started to go camping and that re-introduced me to the stars. I was now at an age where I was thinking about real-world life and career planning with a little more urgency than an eight-year-old. Gazing at the stars still brought me a sense of calm and peacefulness. Then one summer, my friend and I wanted to take our camping to the next level and do something more exciting and adventurous. We went to Colorado to experience some real camping. It was a very pivotal trip for the direction of my life. I was always fascinated by shooting stars and, of course, I would always have to make a wish. I still thought this was the universe's way of asking me what I wanted out of life so it could provide me with an accurate road map for the journey. I still like to think that."

I was totally engaged in his story when customers started to arrive at the store. I desperately wanted to keep the closed sign up and just keep going, but I had bills to pay. The story would just have to wait.

I couldn't get the story out of my head for the rest of the day. I had a million questions I wanted to ask him, but I knew if I did, I wouldn't be satisfied with only bits and pieces at a time. So, I had to wait. Patience is definitely not one of my virtues. His story became a kind of epic tale that continued on each day before and after hours. I would spend my time during the day and after Brad left contemplating the lessons of his stories. I would call that my homework. The next day, I would go to work prepared with a whole new list of questions to ask. They were questions about his experiences, his lessons learned, what would he would do over again, and which ones of his shooting-star wishes had come true. It was all so fascinating to me and made a lot of sense. My desire to learn more was growing exponentially. There never was enough time to get the story finished. It was a perpetual cliffhanger; I always stayed tuned in for the next episode.

What wasn't quite so obvious during this time was that my attraction to Brad was growing. I was completely comfortable being around him and I wanted to be around him all the time. I was even becoming jealous when he had to leave and go back to his "real home" and Emily. I had to absorb everything I could with whatever time I could get with him. When he was with me, my eyes would be glued to his face as I watched and listened to every word that came out of his mouth. Each of those moments brought me a sense of knowing and peace. I never wanted to let any of that go.

Many times, Brad would expand on his story of the Colorado trip. He told tell me that each year he went on these "vision quests." They were his "pilgrimage" to reconnect with the stars for reflection on his journey: past, present, and future. He told me about each of his quests and the influence they had on his life. I felt like I was living inside a movie—close enough to be real, along with the intrigue of an experience just out of reach of reality. His tales kept me hanging on to the desire to complete my journey and reach my destination. I was beginning to understand what Brad kept saying about us each having our own journey and destination.

The more I thought about it, the more I realized I'd been trying to reach his destination. Now, I wanted my own destination. I was finally comprehending how to recognize my own destination and follow my own map. It was exciting, challenging, and fulfilling. But there was one problem: my lack of patience was always one step ahead of me. I was constantly thinking about how to learn more and what I needed to do next to achieve that. It wasn't long before the answer was clear, at least to me.

We were having one of our sessions when he mentioned that this year's vision quest was coming up. Yes, my thoughts immediately went there—I was going to go. Even though he didn't directly invite me, just bringing it up was the universe's way of telling me what that next step was. I wasn't quite sure how I was going to make it happen, but they didn't call me Mack for nothing. I didn't say anything about the universe's order for me to go with him, but I started slipping in a few subtle questions about his own plans for the trip. I didn't want to be to bold about that because it was his trip, after all, and it was very personal to him. I wanted to avoid putting him in the awkward position of saying no (or yes for that matter) to my request to tag along. I also didn't want to put myself in the position of hearing no and having my excitement (and heart) crushed. When it first popped into my head it honestly wasn't about an intimate rendezvous—or at least that's what I told myself.

But as I was constructing the plan for my impending trip some of the realities started to present themselves, even penetrating through all of the firewalls I'd put up to prevent that from happening. The more I was trying to put that part of the plan together, the more sexually active my thoughts were becoming. Still, I was sure this was the right thing to do and I was confident I was going to make it happen. At this stage, the biggest problem was that I had no idea of when he was going. He offered up no hints on the dates, but I knew it was getting close.

It was the end of the day on a Tuesday when he came to me and said he was going to leave early on Friday and not be at work on Saturday. He hadn't even asked his boss. I froze with panic about what to do—not about the store, but about me tagging along on his trip. I had to think fast and make a decision. I decided to buy just a little more time, so I told him that there was no problem with him taking the time off.

That night, I couldn't eat or sleep, let alone make any decisions. My racing thoughts kept jumping back and forth between a hot and sensual spa weekend and Brad freaking out and never coming back to me. The next day, I still had no idea what I was going to do. I must have been pretty quiet because Brad asked me a couple of times if everything was alright. I conceded to myself that not being able to make a decision was my decision. By this time, it was too late to go anyway. I went from being frantic and desperate to quiet and depressed. I'm sure that was what Brad was picking up on. We didn't stay late that night or the next because he had to get things ready for his trip. That depressed me even more because it suddenly felt like our relationship was being put on hold, again. I guessed I just needed to move on. All the plans were in place and Brad would be on his vision quest and I would be working at the store all by myself. I cried myself to sleep that night.

I woke up in the morning feeling better. Everything was set, so I figured I'd finally accepted what was to be. Then I saw the horoscope that had spoken to me before, which I had cut and taped onto my bathroom mirror. *Keep pursuing the truth,* it said. The truth was that I wanted to go on this vision quest with Brad, so that is what I was going to do. It was Brad who taught me that when I'd asked him about going to church with my family. "Go because you want to go for your dad" is what he'd told me. Now I was going to go because I wanted to go for me. I had to come up with a plan, and fast, for that to happen. I didn't waste any time. I decided to do something else Brad taught me: trust my gut.

When I got to the store that morning, I was in an extremely good mood. Brad was noticeably puzzled. How had I gone from being so quiet and distant the day before to so jubilant and upbeat today? I think it was about noon when I asked him what time he was going to leave and he said around two. Then it just came out. "Can I go?" That moment just froze for what seemed like an eternity. I wasn't sure I wanted life to go on at that moment. I don't recall what his reaction was because I was so wrapped up with my own state of mind.

He then replied, very matter of factly, "I guess there's no reason why not."

"Then let's go." I immediately put the closed sign on the door and grabbed my already packed bag out of the truck. I didn't want to give him any opportunity to change his mind. I don't think it would have mattered because it was long after two o'clock before he came out of his shocked trance.

Once we were on the road, it hit me that I hadn't even thought about what he was going to do about Emily. At first, I felt bad, but then I started to wonder if Brad not saying anything about Emily was a good thing or not. Was he doing what everyone told me men do? Was he sneaking around on his wife? Was he expecting this to be something sexual? Was I? Was it all going to be my fault because I'd seduced him into taking me? That internal conversation ended quicker than it began. Nothing about our relationship was normal, so why would this be? I'd been continuing to learn to trust my gut and it was telling me not to worry. I was clearly on my journey, which had so many different possibilities as a final destination point. I'd never been so excited in my entire life. I had no idea about what was going to happen next. It had to be good, right? All of a sudden, I broke out of my reverie when I heard him say, "What are you going to tell Jessie?"

Oops, I had forgotten to tell Brad that Jessie and I were no longer together. In a matter-of-fact sort of way, I said, "Oh, didn't I tell you that we split up?" I did notice a reaction this time because it stayed on his face for quite a while. It kind of made me giggle (on the inside I hope).

Chapter 23

I WASN'T SURE HOW LONG THE TRIP WAS TO WHEREV-er it was that we were going. I'm guessing it was an hour, or maybe two, before Brad blurted out, "When were you going to tell me about you and Jessie?" He didn't sound mad, but he didn't sound like he was happy either. I wouldn't have blamed him regardless. I had never seen Brad get mad about anything. That was one of the things it took me a long time to recognize but when I did, I knew it was one of the things that drew me to him. I was worried that there was a first time for everything—and this could be that time—and I had to admit I would have deserved it. He listened to me very intently without saying a word while I told him the whole story. I told him about the conversations I had with my mom and dad. I didn't leave out any details. When I was done, he asked me about my conversa-tions with Jessie. Hmm, that kind of stumped me. I hadn't even noticed that Jessie had been omitted from my explanation.

As I started to construct the words in my head to explain the Jessie part of the story, it occurred to me that I was looking like the bad one, the one at fault. It was the first time I really saw it that way. I never thought Jessie was a bad guy or even at fault about our relationship not working, but I never even considered that I would come off as looking like the bad guy. I finally just told Brad that we had both agreed that our marriage wasn't working and it was better if we just moved on with our lives.

Surprisingly, that seemed to be enough for Brad. He didn't even try to dig deeper into the heart of the matter. That was very unusual for Brad because he dug deep into everything, even the reason why they put the peanuts in the Peanut Buster Parfaits the way they do. Brad was more interested in the dynamics that occurred between my mom and dad and me. He asked me a lot of questions about what I was thinking and feeling about everything. Answering his questions made me see just how far I had come on my journey already. Just the very fact that I was talking so openly about everything—well almost everything—with my parents and him showed tremendous growth. The conversation ended with Brad asking me how I was feeling now. I told him I was feeling good. Then I smiled while thinking to myself that that was the truth. He simply said, "Good."

What followed was a total shift of direction. He asked, "Will you go out with me?"

"What? Huh? What did you say?" I hadn't seen that coming!

He repeated, "Will you go out with me?"

"I'm not sure. We don't like the same kind of dates."

"I am willing to compromise."

"Then alright, I'll go out with you."

Referring to a previous lighthearted comment I'd made about us dating, he remarked, "I guess one of the mysteries of the universe has been solved." I knew right then we were going to have a good weekend.

My question about whether Brad and I would have enjoyed dating each other was answered. He was in rare form about us going on this date. I'd told him previously that I liked traditional dates such as a nice dinner and a movie. I also told him that I expected to get flowers, too. That was a tongue-in-cheek response to his previously declared dislike of those kinds of traditional dates.

"In order to be a gentleman, I have decided I will compromise what I thought was appropriate for a first date for what I think my date will find pleasing."

What the hell does that mean?

What it meant was I was going to have the best date and most hilarious day of my life at the same time! We went to a dive of a restaurant, a 1970s drive-in movie musical, and he bought me flowers from a gas station. I laughed and cried the entire night. Everything felt very natural, comfortable, and perfect. I was having so much fun that I didn't even think about what was going to happen when the date part of the evening was over.

We got to our campsite shortly after midnight. It was a beautiful night, so we didn't even bother to set up the tent. We talked a little about a lot of things. We did talk about some heavy stuff like God, but those conversations didn't make me so uneasy anymore. It was almost like the separation from general topics to deep topics was becoming very transparent and fading away. Words could not adequately express this moment, lying there under the stars with Brad, no words necessary, no other place to be. Not once through this whole weekend did I think about anything other than what was going on with Brad and me. I think I believed that this was what life was going to be like from now on. I felt like I had actually reached my sought-after destination.

I woke up the next morning and slowly adjusted to the new day and sunlight. I thought, *We made it through the first night.* Now we were about to spend our first day together that was not at the store. We could no longer call ourselves just "work friends." Would that change anything? The day turned out to be very simple. There was no rushing around, no appointments to meet, no shopping to do, and nothing that "had to be done." I couldn't remember if I'd ever experienced a day like that. I was relaxed and happy. I found myself able to just appreciate the world around me. As we toured the town, which didn't take long, we took our time and I saw the small shops with a new perspective. When we went into the shops, I took the time to actually talk to the owners and ask them questions. I always asked them if they were happy. Surprisingly, they all said they were. They would tell me, all with different words, that working as a small shop owner in a small town allowed them to work to live, instead of living to work. I felt they all recognized the importance and value that should be our driving force, which was the same driving force I was looking for. I was seeing it firsthand and I could see it working. Now if I could just put it in a bottle and take it with me, I would be happy.

After our stroll through town and the shops, we went to a local park. The same sense of peace followed me there. We talked, we had a picnic, and then we talked some more. Our conversations were now easy and free flowing, without any concerns about what topics to talk about or worries that the feelings we were sharing were exposing our inner vulnerabilities. I started to wonder if this was all part of Brad's teaching curriculum. Was this him taking me on a field trip? I thought there was no way, because he had been given no time to put all of this together, but it was still weird how the whole date thing came together. It really didn't matter, though—I was learning a lot regardless of how it came to be.

For the rest of the day, nothing eventful happened, but it still was wonderful. It was an experience I would never forget. This day was very simple in its definition, but it was very engaging in its scope. As the evening was fading and we started to head back to the campsite, I was not experiencing any anxiety like I had been the night before. I was ready for the encore of the previous night's star show and I was really looking forward to another night with Brad. I didn't have any expectations for the night but only an anticipation of more of the same. That would be good enough for me.

We got ourselves settled in to watch the spectacle. We both seemed relaxed. Normally, I would have been a bit tired from all of the walking we did and a full day of activity, but I was actually more energized. As we were lying there, the stars began to shoot across the sky. Neither of us said much. I attributed that to just taking in the show. Then I started to wonder what Brad was thinking. So, I asked him. I told him to be totally honest with me. For some strange reason, I wasn't afraid of what his answer might be. I knew whatever he said was going to be good—it always was. But then I started to worry because he was hesitating, for more than just a brief moment. Was I in for a major crash? It was difficult to see the expression on his face because it was dark. It felt very serious though. He finally began to talk, and it was different than the tone of our past conversations. He was talking to me in a way I had never heard, and it was scaring me.

"So much has happened to me in the last year that I don't know where to begin. But the most significant thing has been you. I have learned a lot—a lot about people, life, and myself. I am scared. I am scared about not knowing what is going to happen next, scared about you and me, scared about Emily, scared about losing everything. But what has kept me going is you. I don't know how or why I ended up in your store that day. I don't know why I kept going back. I don't know what I expected from you or what I wanted from you. All I do know is that I'm so grateful that you were there and continue to be there. I've never felt this way about anyone. I didn't even know I could feel this way. Don't get me wrong—I love Emily. She is a very special person who has loved me unconditionally. But she doesn't get me to the same place as you do. That isn't anybody's fault; it's just another mystery of the universe. There's a term that people use to describe how deeply in love they are: soul mates. I always wanted to believe that there truly was such a thing, but every time I thought I found someone who said they'd met their soul mate, it turned out not to be true. I finally came to accept that no such thing existed. That is until

I met you. I can't even say exactly what it is that makes me feel that way about you, but I just do. You're young enough to be my daughter and you come from a completely different background and culture. We're from different generations, but I can't imagine a life without you. But I also can't imagine a life where we could be together. You asked me to tell you the truth and I have. The most precious thing we have is the truth and the second is time. I don't want to miss out on the truth by letting time get away from me. You've been asking me to teach you how to find your peace and I wasn't sure if finding peace can even be taught, but time is precious and that is a lesson that can be taught. There really is only one lesson that you need to master and that is to embrace the truth, and now."

We both sat there in silence for quite some time. I don't know how to describe it but the best I can do is say that my whole being was trembling. I didn't know what to say or do. I had heard the term "soul mates" before but I never really paid any attention to what it meant. Now I knew exactly what it meant. Tears began to well up in my eyes and my heart pounded faster and faster. Finally, I reached over and put my arms around him like I'd never done with anyone before. I still couldn't speak. We both started to lie back down as if on cue. I just did what came naturally at that time and curled up next to him. I put my head on his shoulder and my hand over his heart. His heart was beating at the very same beat as mine. There was nothing more in my life that I wanted. I already had perfection. However, Brad was still looking for his answer about me. Part of me was unbelievably ecstatic over how Brad felt about me. But the other part of me was more scared than

I had ever been in my whole life. Would his answer take him away from me?

We drifted off to sleep and when we awoke it was like coming out of a dream. The dream was now over and everything was going to return to normal. At least the world we would be stepping back into. We packed up our stuff and headed for home. We didn't talk much until we were almost home, and then I think we were both trying to reacclimate ourselves back into reality. When we arrived at the store, he carried my bag over to the truck and started to say good-bye. I grabbed him and pulled him close and kissed him. I wasn't sure if this was going to be a good-bye kiss or a desperate attempt to sway his truth. He didn't resist but he really didn't kiss me back, either. I think I was trying to convince him, and myself, that this was going to be our future, our final destination and that we were going to be together. I couldn't imagine it any other way. I definitely never could have imagined the way it did turn out.

Chapter 24

MY WORLD TOTALLY COLLAPSED AFTER MY DAD DIED. Everything had just gotten to a place where I was happy. Now, all of that was gone, and I had no one to go through it all with. My dad was gone, and my mom was suffering through her own grief. I didn't know what was going on with Brad, but it was over—I made sure of that. He was the only person I knew who could get me through all of it, but he was the one I put blame on. He, too, was a part of my loss. There were a lot of people who tried to console me but I knew what I needed to do and no one was going to be able to understand that, let alone be able to do it for me. Brad had taught me a new way to deal with things like this and I thought I had understood it, but that was because Brad made it easy. It was a totally different story navigating through it by myself. Especially when I didn't have the energy or the will to even try. I only wanted to find a reason why, a reason to blame someone, someone like Brad. I spiraled down into a deep depression. It was the darkest time of my life and I saw no way out. I couldn't even get myself to go and talk to my closest confidants, Sunshine and Lady.

I went to work every day hoping that it might keep my mind off all the horror that was going on in my life. It didn't work. All around me were memories of Brad. There was the picnic table where we sat and ate lunch every day, the counter where we had our first conversation, our first touch. Worst of all was going to the back office where I'd surprised Brad with his birthday party and present. I didn't know why I couldn't just pick up the phone and call him or at least send him a text. I was angry that he hadn't called me but I also knew that it was my own fault. I never wanted to admit it, Brad knew exactly what he was doing by not calling me and that this was another lesson I needed to learn even though I felt like I was done learning lessons. There was still a part of me that thought that if I caved in and called him, I would be failing this lesson. There was nothing I wanted to put any effort into except being angry. I was numb. I was defeated. I was done caring about anything. I didn't care about truth anymore, so I just kept running away from it. One thing I still agreed with was that time was precious—but my precious time was gone and I feared I wouldn't get it back, ever.

That atmosphere carried over into every area of my life. What friends I had left never called. My customers stopped coming to the store because my usual sunny disposition had faded. It was probably about a month and a half before my mom started to adjust back into the world on a fragile basis. She started coming into the store. I don't know if she was there to make sure I was okay or to throw her own pity party. Either way, I wasn't interested. I didn't need that because it wasn't going to change anything. What was done was done. The progress I'd made with my mother was all gone. Neither of us wanted to talk about anything, especially Dad. She figured out somehow that I was with Brad the night Dad died but she didn't go there, at least not at first. Maybe she was blaming him, too. He was an easy and convenient target for both of us.

My anger turned into an unbearable sadness at the end of every day. Most of the time I went home to cry myself to sleep, or sometimes even until sunrise. The thoughts kept creeping into my head, telling me that Brad was out there somewhere. Why wasn't he there with me? I became infuriated whenever the conversation about soul mates entered my mind. Where was my soul mate now?! I had no doubt in my mind that Brad had totally abandoned me because he just went back to Emily. It was easy for him to return to his life, his life without me. There were no right answers about anything for me. Logic was a myth. Truth was a lie. Life was hell, not peace.

Sustenance was not important to me. I didn't care if the store was making money or not. I guess I should just say that I didn't care that the store wasn't making any money. I didn't care that without the store making money I couldn't afford my house or to feed Sunshine and Lady—let alone myself—because that didn't matter to me anyway. I couldn't even go talk with Sunshine and Lady. Mom was living off a life insurance policy Dad had from work and her low-paying part-time job. She would try to find a way to share that with me, but she had to survive herself and, apparently, she wanted to stay alive. Mom and Dad had invested all their savings into the store. The bill collectors weren't calling yet, but we knew they would be soon. Of course, I didn't care. Mom started to look for a higher paying and full-time job but wasn't having success. She, and I for that matter, didn't have any real marketable skills or the time and desire to learn any.

Mom was desperately trying to keep the store alive. I think she felt it was a perpetual connection to Dad and she didn't want to let it go. I felt like the store was more of a connection to Brad, and I was trying to break that chain around my neck. It was a tug-of-war battle between my mom and me and neither of us was going to let go of the rope. We became very passive-aggressive with each other and constantly bickered. We were making life miserable. We were no longer trying to do the smart things like selling one of the houses and moving in together to save money. Instead, everything was about who was right, who had the best idea. There was never a winner in these battles. There would be only one way to do things—my way. This would be my life now.

Chapter 25

WE WERE HEADING INTO WINTER AND THE DAYS WERE getting colder and shorter. That didn't help my mood or mind-set in any way. It had been more than three months since my dad died and I had my last encounter with Brad. It felt like it had been hours and yet it felt like it had been years at the same time. I had settled into a state of "just not giving a damn." I think my mom was doing better, but I still was not cooperating with any of my share of the effort. The only thing that I was becoming clearer about was selling the store. It had not gotten any easier going in to work and visiting my memories. I was coming to the realization that the only solution was to get rid of the store before I could even start to think about moving on. The late notices and threats of being turned over to collections were becoming part of my daily mail ritual.

Thanksgiving came and went, I think. There was no family or turkey that I remember. What I did remember was flipping the calendar to the month of December. Without family or even friends and a pretty severe hatred of God, there really wasn't anything to celebrate about Christmas. Even the store was not a very good distraction from all of the holiday cheer. It seemed clear to me in that moment that the beginning of the year would be a good time to start with a clean slate. I would close the store and begin to move on.

Christmas wasn't a big business season for a store like mine. We were more of a spring and summer sort of store and those were way off in the distance. Thinking about that didn't do anything to repair my attitude. Instead, it started me going down the road in the wrong direction. The floodgates opened wide and the flow of the past year came rushing out, flooding my space with another round of anger and hopelessness. My marriage coming to an end, my dad dying, the pending loss of my store, my house, my mom, my horses, and even losing Brad.

For the first time since all of this started, I asked myself, *What am I going to do about this?* It wasn't really an enthusiastic thought, but it did have a hint of hope to it. Then I thought, *What would Brad do?* It took me a moment before I realized what I had actually asked myself. I asked again but this time I really thought about it, seriously thinking about what Brad would do. It was the first time since Brad had been out of my life that I thought about him without becoming angry or depressed. It was also the first time in a very long time I was experiencing a bit of calm. Next, I asked myself what I was going to do instead of what I was going to let happen to me. It wasn't much, but it was a bit of a different kind of thinking. It didn't last long, though, before that ugly evil voice in my head said it was too late. Everything was in motion and I couldn't stop it. I just had to accept what was going to be and stop fooling myself. I would give in to that voice, but I did acknowledge to myself that there was at least a battle starting in my head. But I still wasn't convinced that this was a sign of hope.

Eventually, though, that battle turned into a raging war. I went back and forth between fighting for the future and defending my past. The past was pretty ingrained into my being and it was holding its ground well. That became very apparent one night when my journey took an unexpected turn and I wasn't wearing my seatbelt. Sometimes though, not wearing a seatbelt can actually save your life.

I was working by myself at the store and it was getting near to closing time when a car pulled up. I wasn't in the mood for a customer but that had become true anytime a customer came to the store. The door opened and I was ready to tell the customer that I was closed when I looked up. I couldn't believe who walked in. It was Jessie. The last real interaction I'd had with Jessie was during that same horrible weekend my whole life shattered. In my desperation to go on the trip with Brad, I asked Jessie if he could watch the store for me while I had to go out of town. We had been getting along very amicably as friends and Jessie was trying to play nice, so he'd agreed.

After that tragic weekend, I'd only had a couple of interactions with him. He was at my dad's wake and funeral and gave me his condolences. I was not very reciprocating with the sentiment. I was angry with everyone and that included him, though there wasn't any reason I should've been. He tried calling me once, maybe twice, but I never called him back. He finally left a message saying he wanted to make sure I was alright and to let him know if I needed anything. It was the same thing everybody was saying to me and nothing was special about any of the offers, even his. After that, I didn't hear anything more from Jessie, until now that is.

The war raging in my mind had now turned into chaos. I wanted to hug him and kick his ass at the same time. He didn't deserve either though, and I didn't do either. He politely said, "Hi, Mackenzie. I don't want to bother you, but I saw the lights on and I just wanted to see if you were okay."

That was all it took for me to start to soften up. It was the first time in months I wanted to hug someone. I just never thought it would be Jessie. Him being there took me back to a time when I used to complain about being unfulfilled, but now it felt like a time to which I wanted to return. A time where I had a mom and a dad, a husband, my own store, and home. It was a time that was much simpler and that seemed so appealing to me now.

I started talking to him about what was going on in a very general way. "Yes, I am doing fine. Things are tough, but I'll get through it. Mom's okay . . ." and so on and so forth. Then somewhere along the line, I realized I was having a much more personal conversation with him than I'd ever had before. He was listening very attentively with sincere, heartfelt responses. I looked up at the clock and realized I had been talking for almost an hour. I was kind of embarrassed and blushed when I said, "I'm sorry to go on like that."

"That's okay. Would you like to go get something to eat and catch up on things a little more?"

That sounded really good to me, so I said, "Yes."

We were at the restaurant for several hours. It felt like the date that Jessie and I had never had. I was feeling something about Jessie that had never existed before. The voice in my head was now telling me that I had been a fool for giving up on Jessie. I was reckless in the way I'd handled my life and had let Brad influence me into what was now the life of hell that I'd created.

As we were leaving the restaurant Jessie said to me again, "Let me know if you need anything."

I paused for a moment. "Would you like to come over for a little while?" I could tell that he didn't know what to do, but he couldn't say no.

We sat on the couch at my (our) place for about an hour before he got up to leave. As he was walking toward the door, I stopped him and gave him a hug. It was the first hug I had given to anybody since my dad died. I didn't want to let go of Jessie, or did I mean my past? The next thing I remembered was waking up in the morning lying next to Jessie.

All of a sudden, everything felt wrong again. I wasn't blaming Jessie for anything. This was all on me. I asked myself, *Who am I? What am I doing? Where am I going with my life?* I started to cry. That's when Jessie woke up. He was concerned about why was I crying and kept asking what he could do.

The war that was raging inside my head right before Jessie showed up was starting again. I told Jessie that there was nothing he could do. "Jessie, nothing has changed between you and me. Last night shouldn't have happened. It was a mistake. I'm sorry."

That was when Jessie became upset. Not in an emotional way but in an angry way. He finally let out what he had been holding inside for a long time.

"It's that old man at the store, isn't it?! Ever since he started coming around, you've been acting strange. Did you have an affair with him?!"

"No!" I shouted back. "He was just a good customer who became a friend, that's all!"

I couldn't believe what came out of Jessie's mouth. "So, what are you selling him?!"

Stunned, I screamed, "How dare you say something like that! He is a great guy and a great friend, more than you ever were!"

What he said next made my heart jump out of my chest. "Come on, Mack, everyone knows that you were with him when your dad died. It's no secret."

"What do you mean?" I asked fearfully.

"His wife came to the store that weekend looking for you. She said her husband usually came to the store but he was out of town, so she needed to come and get the cat food. She said that she wanted to meet you. Don't even try to tell me that it was a coincidence that you were both out of town at the same time!"

I didn't know what to say. Did Emily find out about everything? Was that why Brad had completely disappeared from my life? I just wanted to die at that moment. I had thought my life had reached bottom and it couldn't get any worse, but I was wrong: it just got worse. I glared at Jessie, "Just leave."

He gave me a mocking smile, shook his head, and walked out the door. I couldn't believe what had just happened. I couldn't move. I couldn't breathe. I just cried and cried that whole day. I wanted to be with Brad so much at that moment, without any reservations. There was no way that could ever happen again.

The next morning, I woke up still extremely depressed, embarrassed, and feeling hopeless. I had no idea what to do. I decided to just get up and go into the store and start packing things up. I couldn't get it out of my head Jessie saying that everyone knew about Brad and me. Did that mean Emily? My mom? Could it have even meant my dad? I just couldn't handle anything at that moment. Until I remembered Brad had told me that you should only focus on the things that you can control. That sent a brief moment of calm over me. He was right. There was nothing I could do about what happened, but there was something I could do about my life moving forward. Maybe this year was lost, but on January 1, a new one would be starting. That would be a good time for me to start in a new direction. It was time to put this year behind me and put my focus on the future and not the past. What would my dad be thinking about all my sulking and just giving up? He'd spent his whole life teaching me to be tough and push through adversity and do whatever it was I set my mind to. He gave me his money and trusted me to honor him by accomplishing my dreams. He'd believed in me so much—how could I not respect that? How could I even think about giving up? My name was Mack and that was for a reason. I wasn't going to be called Mackenzie anymore.

When I walked out the door that night, I stepped into a cold and crisp winter night. I stopped to take in the moment and looked up at the sky. I couldn't believe what I saw. It was a shooting star. I remembered Brad telling me how a shooting star was the universe's way of asking what you wanted so it could grant you the right wish to get you to your destination. So, I made a wish. That was the first time I'd wished on a shooting star since I'd been with Brad. It was also the first time I went inside myself to find my truth without Brad. It was a good place. I had forgotten about the peace of that place. It was a place that brought back fond and meaningful memories. Maybe that was the lesson Brad was trying to teach me in his absence. At least that's what I told myself.

On the drive home that night, I experienced something I hadn't since my dad had died. I was looking forward to going to work the next day. I also couldn't get the shooting star out of my head. There was something eerily comforting about it. I didn't know why, but it made me smile.

Chapter 26

———

WHEN I WOKE UP THE NEXT MORNING, I WAS STILL looking forward to going to work. I got all my stuff together and I even left about an hour earlier than usual. I hadn't done that since Brad and I would go in early to talk. The nostalgia must have played tricks on my mind. When I pulled into the store, I was expecting to see Brad's car. He always got there before me and he loved to give me a hard time about not getting there before the help. That was a bad example for the boss to set. I was disappointed when I came back to reality. Brad had been on my mind since I saw the shooting star the previous night. I felt good that I could think of him without getting angry and upset.

I went into the store and contemplated what to do. Again, my mind was in the past, so I was thinking like I had when the store was flourishing. I had to shake off those cobwebs and get real again. As I was pulling the boxes off the shelf in the back, I bent the flaps back to take a look inside. I came to the shelves that held the boxes of Christmas decorations. I opened the first box and all I could do was sit there and stare. Slowly, I started taking the ornaments out one by one. I couldn't put them up since we were going to be out of business in a couple of weeks and it wouldn't make any sense. Then, I thought I wasn't going to need them anyway, so why didn't I just put them up for sale in the going-out-of-business sale?

I continued to take them out of the boxes, but with each one, I had to stop and re-live the story behind it. I had a lot of decorations to go through, but I was finally able to start having some good memories of Christmases past. I used to love Christmas and even though I wasn't very religious, I still liked to decorate for the holidays. I realized that this was going to take forever, but it didn't matter. I went right back to admiring each decoration with no urgency to speed up the process. When my mom got to the store that morning, she was surprised to see me there already. Then, she raised her eyebrows and asked what I was doing. I thought it was pretty obvious. "Getting ready for Christmas," I said.

Her expression didn't change. I am sure she thought I'd finally lost it all. I pulled out the next ornament and my mom sat down next to me and started to tell me the story behind the ornament. Then the next one, and then another and another. We didn't realize what time it was until it became dark. We hadn't even turned the lights on that day. We'd spent the whole day looking at ornaments. Those moments were also the first real civil moments between Mom and me since Dad had died.

I had heard how people go through different stages when experiencing grief. Maybe I was entering a stage that wasn't going to be so horrible. I could only hope. At the end of the day

I also realized that I wasn't apprehensive about whether or not my mom actually knew about Brad and me. If she did, she certainly didn't let on that she did. Getting through this first day dealing with that was a big deal. I didn't need to worry about whether she knew or not. There was nothing I could do about it anyway. I just wanted to move on.

The next day continued on in the same manner. The only difference was our mood was slowly shifting from somber to a fond remembrance. Our stories were bringing back a sense of our family spirit.

With things getting back on track with my mom, I decided to ask her a question about something that had happened a while back. The opportunity for this conversation had never happened until now. "Why did Dad start going back to church?" I wasn't sure if Mom even had a clue. I'm not even sure there was an answer, but I needed to at least ask. To my amazement, Mom had an answer. Not just an opinion or an idea, she actually knew the reason. She appeared to be excited about the chance to talk with me about that subject. She told me later that she thought we'd never be able to have that kind of conversation in our lives again considering the way things were going. She also said that she felt it was important for me to know why. Then without any hesitation she began to talk.

"Your father lived for you. Nothing mattered more to him than his little cowgirl. He admittedly couldn't let go of taking care of you. He took great pride in raising you to be able to take care of yourself but that didn't take away his desire to fight the fight for you—not because he didn't think you could handle it, but just because he wanted to. I'm sure you remember that when things broke down between you and Jessie your father was very much in control of his emotions."

Yes, I did remember his response very clearly because it wasn't at all what I could have even imagined.

Mom continued, "That was because he trusted you and knew that you were totally capable of taking care of your business. I never said anything to your father about what was going on between you and Jessie, but he knew. As difficult as it was for him to stay out of it, he knew he needed to let you be you and take care of it yourself."

I was feeling so proud of my father, and myself. He had recognized who I was, and I recognized the lessons I'd learned from him. The thought of giving my dad a big hug in that moment reminded me of the hole I had in my heart.

Next, Mom began to talk about the different reaction my dad had about the situation with Brad, without me even asking. Somehow, she knew what I was thinking. She was right. She continued, "The concern your father had about all of that wasn't about Brad, or even you. It was about him. He trusted you. He knew without a doubt that you could handle yourself with anybody, Jessie or Brad. The difference was that he saw Jessie's role to be a shared and supportive role, an extension of his role. On the other hand, Brad was a father-like figure, and that was treading on his territory. He was afraid that Brad was replacing him and that you didn't need him anymore. That was something he couldn't handle. Your father was not very good at expressing his feelings through words, so he reacted in the only way he could, through his raw emotions."

My thoughts went back to my initial question, "What does any of this have to do with him wanting to go back to church?"

Acting as if she hadn't even heard me ask, she went on, "I didn't have any idea that any of these things were connected. One Friday night, we were eating dinner. Out of nowhere, he said that we were going to church on Sunday and he asked me to call and invite you to go with us. Although he used the word 'invite' it sounded more like a directive. I stopped chewing and just looked at him until he asked, 'Is there a problem with that?' I just said, 'No' and resumed dinner. Going to church went on like it was—and had been—a part of our normal family routine. It wasn't until the week before he passed that we talked about it. He took me to the park to go for a walk. Just the two of us. We hadn't done anything like that since before you were born. That was when he shared everything with me. I'd never heard your father talk like that. He was articulate, sensitive, and sincere. I couldn't even say anything myself because I was in a state of awe. I didn't need to say anything or even ask any questions because he said everything. His words came out effortlessly and completely, but it did not feel scripted." My mother went on to describe my father's story.

"When everything started to happen regarding Brad and having him help out at the store, your father began to unravel. Like I said before, he was feeling like you didn't need him anymore. Even though Brad was an easy target, he wasn't the driving force behind what was happening to your father. The root cause came from his feeling that he no longer had anything to teach you. He even used the classic line that the 'student had become the teacher.' As a parent, you never want to have the feeling that there is nothing left in life to share with your kids. His whole being was empty. He was so very proud of you and the person you had become. He told me that you had achieved more than he ever dreamed possible. Then he stopped for a moment before he said that he had nothing left to give.

"Then, like a teenager excited about going off to college or embarking on a new career, he started to talk about church. He said that he noticed something was different about his little girl, something special that had taken over and was making her strong and so smart about life, about everything. He went on to say how something like that must have come from God and he wanted to understand it. He wanted to learn all about it. He wanted what he saw in you, Mackenzie. A peace, a glow about life. He thought that by you going to church with us you could help him discover whatever it was.

"He didn't know how to explain all of this to you or how to ask you for your help. A parent goes through their entire life caring for their children until the point when the child has to take over for the care of their parent. It's one of the most difficult transitions that a person has to make. As a parent, you're never ready for that, never prepared. Your father certainly wasn't ready for that transition. I asked him why he was telling me all of this. His reply was prophetic. He said that if anything happened to him, he wanted to make sure I could tell you thank you for helping him realize what was important in life. He said he was feeling good about things and that he was attributing that to you. Your strength and confidence when dealing with his and your emotional exchange had made him see what the most precious things in life were—spending time with the ones you love and most of all, trusting the ones you love. He smiled, he kissed me, and then he said he loved me. We had the most wonderful time of our life before he passed. That time will be the most precious time that I will have forever." Mom started to cry, but it was a good cry. Then, I started to cry. It was a good cry, too.

After listening to that story, it was very easy for me to reconcile the anger I'd been feeling and acting upon after losing my dad. I no longer felt like lashing out; instead, I felt like celebrating knowing who my dad truly was. I was ready to start moving forward.

We stopped focusing on closing the store and the pending gloom and doom of our future. We still had to face what was to come but I was getting my soul back. I was getting my "Mack"-attack drive back, too. I kept wondering, though, if it was just too late.

I also was seriously thinking about calling Brad. He'd gotten me through the early days of the store, and I knew he could get me through this. My perspective concerning Brad had changed. I was no longer angry at him or blaming him for everything, or anything for that matter. It wasn't his fault that my dad had died. I couldn't blame him for my decision to leave Jessie. Quite the opposite, I was the happiest I had ever been in my life when I was with Brad. Besides, I'm sure he had moved on with his life and wanted nothing to do with me anymore after what I'd said to him. Or maybe Emily finding out had something to do with his disappearance. I would just have to find a way to get through all of this on my own, at least for now.

Chapter 27

I WAS NOT PREPARED FOR WHAT HAPPENED NEXT, BUT then again, I didn't believe there was any way to prepare for such an event. It had been a week since I started coming into work early again. Each day when I pulled into the parking lot, I would have that same moment of hope that Brad would be sitting in his car waiting for me. Then I would return to reality and the disappointment would set in again.

On this particular day when I pulled into the store parking lot, there was Brad's car! My heart started to pound vigorously, and I couldn't catch my breath. I wondered if my brain was playing tricks on me again, but there was no other reality for me to return to. This truly was happening! Brad was here! Everything was going to be alright! I couldn't wait to see him again, so I jumped out of my truck and started to run toward his car. I was so happy that I was going to give him the biggest and tightest hug in the history of the world! The thought of him being angry or not responding to my excitement did not even cross my mind. Neither did seeing some woman step out of the car and look at me as if I was a lunatic about to attack her. I came to a sudden stop along with my heart. I couldn't believe that this was another hallucination. It had seemed so real. The fact was that it was very real. It just was not the reality I was hoping for.

We both stood there for what felt like an hour before the woman asked, "Are you Mackenzie?"

"Yes," I replied.

"Hi. I'm Emily, Brad's wife."

Absolutely no words existed to describe the thoughts, emotions, fear, and shock that engulfed my whole entire being. This woman never truly existed in my mind. She was just a character in the fictional life of Brad.

I have no idea how long I stood there before she spoke again and asked, "Can we talk?"

There was only one answer to that question, so I said, "Sure."

She did not appear to be carrying a weapon or to be a woman scorned with anger and rage. Actually, she was just the opposite, quiet and polite. It seemed as though she was trying to make every effort to put me at ease, but I could not come up with any possible scenario that there could be a positive outcome. I had no question in my mind that the reason for Emily's visit had everything to do with finding out about the weekend rendezvous between Brad and me that everybody knew about. It was now going to be the moment of truth. I was just going to have to live up to the truth and accept the consequences. It was the only thing I could do.

Obviously, the atmosphere was awkward and tense. She had a good reason to be there, but it appeared she was having trouble finding the right words to begin the conversation. There was no need for small talk or general niceties. I still had no words and no explanation for where I knew this meeting was going.

Finally, Emily began to speak. She took a deep breath and then said, "Brad asked me if I would deliver this gift to you."

I noticed she was carrying a bag with her and I was completely confused as to why Brad would have Emily deliver me a gift. With a puzzled look on my face and a tone of cautious intrigue, I asked, "Is Brad okay?"

Again, Emily took a deep breath, collected her composure, and said, "Brad passed away."

That was the moment the world stopped for me, again. I thought to myself, *Is this a cruel joke she is playing on me for my relationship with Brad?* I needed to know more so I asked her, "What happened?"

She went on to say, "Brad had been diagnosed with terminal cancer back in February and the doctor gave him six months to live. He didn't want anybody to know because he didn't want people to feel sorry for him and treat him differently."

Immediately my mind went back to that time, trying to remember what had been going on with us. It would have been around Valentine's Day. I was so self-absorbed with what was going on with Jessie and me that I didn't even think about anything else that was going on around me. Brad was always the one leading me through those moments to get *me* through. I was totally oblivious to anything that *he* was going through.

Emily then said, "He went peacefully, but before he died, he told me that there was a package he wanted me to give to you. I promised him I would. He told me that I could look at it because he had nothing to hide or feel ashamed about. I didn't look, though. It was between Brad and you."

It was at that point that I felt I really needed to say something: the truth. I started by saying, "Nothing ever happened between us, at least from Brad. We kissed twice but it was me who kissed him. It wasn't his fault. He was always a gentleman who respected me and loved you."

She stopped me there and told me that she wasn't upset or there to pick a fight with the other woman. "I am here to share the truth, the truth I learned from Brad."

For some reason, this was the moment that I really started to get all choked up. My eyes were welling up with tears, my stomach was all knotted up, and my heart felt like it was literally broken into a thousand pieces. It was at this moment that I sensed a connection with Emily beginning and any fear I had was fading away. I still didn't understand everything that was happening or why, but I wanted to hear more of what Emily had to say. She was no longer a fictional character in Brad's story or even "the other woman." She was the last link I had to Brad. I asked her if she could tell me about the truth she'd learned from Brad.

She started to smile and her eyes were welling up with tears, "I would love to." Without hesitation she began telling me her story.

"I was married to Brad for over twenty-seven years and I don't regret one day of it. Each day was easy with him because he always listened and respected my thoughts and feelings about everything. Of course, we didn't agree on everything, but even when we didn't, we never fought or got angry with each other. We were able to learn and grow from our differences and that gave us freedom to live our lives independently yet together. This allowed us to see the world from a whole other perspective than most people. We were able to maintain our own identities yet share the truths each of us was learning along our own paths. It took me most of the twenty-seven years to recognize and understand how precious that was. I resisted it all at first because it didn't make sense to me and it went against so much of common social ideology, but whenever Brad discussed his thoughts and perspective, it continued to intrigue me and make sense to me. Plus, I trusted Brad and he never gave me any reason not to. As time passed, I was paying more attention to the things Brad was saying because he was always right. Not only was everything starting to make sense, but I started to feel uneasy whenever my thinking re-engaged back to the socially accepted norms. I learned to trust my gut because it was always right. There were the times when I still would get upset, jealous, or angry about things, but I knew inside that was my own insecurities and the truth was there to tell me that there was no need for me to feel that way. The better I became at listening to my truth, the easier it was for me to deal with those situations, allowing me to live with peace. Once you experience living in peace, life makes more sense and you live in true happiness."

It was as if I was listening to Brad himself. The words she used and the message she was telling me felt like she was channeling Brad's next lesson to me. It reminded me of how my conversations with Brad always comforted me. It had been so long since I felt that way, but the feeling was back in a big way.

Like I had with Brad, I just wanted to sit quietly and listen to every word Emily had to say. She continued sharing her story:

"A few years ago, Brad wanted to disengage with the world. He wanted to leave his job and pursue his dream of becoming a writer. I was against it at first because it meant changing our whole standard of living and I liked where our life was. He didn't care much about money. His freedom and personal space were what was important to him. I was terrified of cutting our income in half and risking all of the security we had worked so hard to achieve. He told me that we wouldn't do it if I didn't want him to. He told me I didn't even have to give him a reason—I could just say no and that would be the end of story. I listened to my gut and told him it was okay. It was the right decision. I was worried for quite some time because he wasn't doing much. He slipped into an apathetic place. I could tell he was frustrated and upset that I had given up everything I wanted so he could pursue his dream of becoming a writer. It hit its peak around his fiftieth birthday nearly two years ago. He was depressed about the big five-oh and I was starting to feel the strain on our family finances. We never talked about it, but I'm pretty sure we both knew something had to change or we would be heading for trouble.

"Then, slowly things started to change. I noticed that his energy was picking up and his mind was engaging in something. Brad was a deep thinker, but I hadn't seen this in him for quite some time. He never talked about what he was thinking until he had thoroughly processed his thoughts, but the fact that he was thinking again was a good sign to me. I noticed the biggest change when he gave me a kitten for an anniversary present. I had always wanted pets, but he was allergic to most animals—I had just given up on thinking having a pet was ever going to happen. This kitten brought a whole new level of energy into our lives. He was even more enamored and excited by the kitten than I was. From that point on, he seemed like he was always in a good mood and his mind was very active. I knew I had to go back to trusting the initial feeling I had in my gut and give this writing thing some more time.

"This upbeat mood continued up until just a couple of months ago, but that could have had something to do with the cancer. Before that, whenever there was a hint of the mood fading, he would come home with another pet. It was pretty clear that they were for him, but he never would admit to that. I didn't care why because I loved them all too, and if it was helping him then it was just a nice side effect. I did find that the names that he chose for them were kind of strange for pet names. The first one he named Ben. Then there was Bert and then Bob. When he brought the puppy home, he had named him Joe. I asked him where these names were coming from and he would just say they came from a happy place. Then he'd just laugh."

Emily paused and looked at me with a smile. Then it hit me. Oh my God! Those were the names I used to call Brad mistakenly on purpose! All except for Joe. Who was Joe? Then I just busted out laughing. Groundhog Joe was a stuffed animal I was selling at the store on Groundhog Day. Brad had found it strange that I wasn't selling any Valentine's Day stuff, but I was selling stuff for Groundhog Day. Emily was laughing right along with me. She knew, but it felt really good to be able to share it with her.

The tone of our conversation changed dramatically. We started to openly share stories of our time with Brad. We both had a lot of stories. She told me about the early days with her and Brad and I talked about things in a chronological manner. The progression of our relationship was what made the stories interesting, even to me. As I was telling my story, I flew right through my surprise birthday party for Brad without even thinking about what I was saying and to whom I was saying it, until after I let it all out.

All of a sudden, I just stopped and gasped. Feeling horrible, I looked at Emily and said, "I'm sorry, I went too far."

Emily had a smile on her face, "It's okay, I know all about it. Please go on."

I smiled and kept right on going. Boy, this woman was something special. I didn't think twice when it came time to share the vision quest trip, including the date. As I was excitedly telling her about going to the drive-in movie to see *Grease*, my thoughts were running ahead to what had happened next. My excitement was melting back into fear and panic. I told myself I couldn't go there. Then I just stopped again.

I was trembling when Emily reached over and grabbed my hand, "I know about that, too. It's all okay."

When Emily said it was all okay is when the surreal dream came crashing back down to earth. "How could it all be okay?" I blurted out. "How could it all be okay that you're talking to the woman who your husband called his soul mate? How can that be okay?" I did not believe there was any honest answer I could ever accept.

When she started to talk again, Emily returned to the tone she'd had at the beginning of our conversation. "For as far back as I can remember, there was one thing that Brad could not understand but was determined to get answered. He wondered why societal consensus tells us to love each other but we are not taught what that means. He felt that the world presented love in this convoluted smorgasbord of religion, sex, desire, and self-definition. Brad did not like complex and complicated concepts. He was always searching for a simple and easily understood definition. He spent years contemplating, praying, and meditating for his answers. He was going to keep persevering until his gut told him to stop. He would read books and study different religions that told us that they knew what love was. He became very frustrated with religion and he eventually stopped going to church, but he did take one thing with him—the love chapter from the Bible. You know: love is patient, love is kind, and love never fails. That still wasn't enough. One day, by chance, he opened up a dictionary and looked up the word 'love.' It was defined as 'a deep affection for something.' The combination of those two definitions gave him the satisfaction he was looking for. He did not ever believe that sex was the prime indicator or gauge of love but more of an experience of a deep affection between two people. Sex was still biology, and biology was science, and science was based on fact. Love was not fact, and love was not science. It was something that cannot be defined in the same manner."

I wasn't sure where Emily was going with all of this. There was no sex between Brad and me and there had been no talk on the matter with Emily up to now. I wanted to get to the point of this, so I asked her what she was trying to tell me.

"Keep listening," she said. "Brad felt that affection was something beautiful and natural in its purist form. It frustrated him that once a person was married it was no longer acceptable to have intimate relationships with other people of the opposite sex. He used to say, 'What happened to loving each other? Can love only be between two people and limited only to people who are married? Once we are married, are we just supposed to stop loving everybody else?' The whole thing really bothered him because it didn't make sense to him. He didn't talk about his thoughts on this subject because he felt that they were too controversial and people wouldn't understand or even try to understand. He told me he had been thinking about this subject for a long time before he even talked to me about it. I have to admit, I thought it was way out there myself, but I continued to think about what he was saying and gave it a chance. He had a way of drawing me in to topics like that. The longer I thought about it, the more sense it made to me. The one thing I struggled with was the word 'intimate.' When I asked him what exactly that meant he said the term had nothing to do with sex. It simply meant a deep relationship between two people. Within an intimate relationship comes trust, with trust comes truth, and with truth comes peace. When that intimacy is broken so is the trust and then the truth is compromised.

"You asked me how all of this can be okay. Here is my answer. I loved Brad and I know he loved me. He never stopped demonstrating his love to me. From that came the trust, which became the truth. The truth is I am happy and at peace. The truth is Brad was happy and at peace. It is okay to be happy and have peace."

During that part of the conversation where she spoke of intimacy and trust, my mind went to the weekend Brad and I went on our vision quest. Again, I couldn't decide whether to go there with Emily. This deep and open discussion was going well, and I felt that there was a connection happening between us. Did I want to risk all of that by bringing that weekend into play? What did it really matter in the bigger scheme of things? It turned out, it didn't matter what I was thinking, because before I could decide what to do, Emily spoke up.

"You're thinking about the weekend you and Brad went away together, aren't you?"

I hadn't seen that coming. But since she'd brought it up, I guessed that door was open, so I walked through. "Yes."

Emily did not hesitate. She started talking again. "Yes, like I said, I know about that, too. Brad called me the night you left. He told me what was going on and that he didn't want me to worry. I didn't, because Brad had earned my trust and I had learned to trust my intuition. I have never known my intuition to be wrong. The details weren't important to me and we never went there. I'd learned to understand that bond of intimacy Brad talked about. Of course, he had it right. I knew and believed in Brad and if it was important for Brad to be with you then it was important to me. I'm not saying it was easy. Jealousy is an evil intrusion to our being. That is minimized by understanding and it gave me the strength to get through it."

"If you knew I was with Brad that weekend then why did you come by the store?"

"I don't really know. Maybe I thought I could pick up some sort of feeling. I needed to be part of what was going on and that was the only thing I could think of to do."

"And did it help?"

"Yes, it did. I met your husband and we started up a conversation. He seemed confused and very uneasy about talking to me. I think, at first, it was just because I was a customer who was talking to him and talking back was out of his comfort zone. After the conversation continued, I think he started to sense something different. I introduced myself, saying my husband was a regular patron of the store but he was out of town, so I was doing his shopping. A moment later, it was like shattering glass. He got why he was feeling the way he was. I could tell that he was becoming angrier by the minute and wanted to lash out, but he didn't. He probably realized that there really wasn't anything he could say. Maybe it was just because he couldn't make any sense out of this whole matter. We made our exiting salutations and I left. After that, I was just fine. Oh, there was one piece of intimate detail that Brad shared with me: the date." She smiled and I just laughed.

It was just like talking to Brad. He could always take an abstract or totally bizarre situation and make sense out of it, then finish with a touch of humor. Emily was only the second person I had ever known to be able to do that.

It felt like the conversation had run its course. What else was there left to say? We had been talking since early that morning and it was already dark outside. It had been a very emotionally draining day and I was exhausted. I couldn't really describe the wide range of emotions I was feeling, but it was nothing bad. I felt a bit of disappointment that there was no one I would be able to share this whole experience with who would truly understand. It appeared to me that Emily was at the same place, tired, and all of her words had been used up. I started feeling sad that this day was coming to an end and that I had no idea what was going to happen next on my journey. Would I ever see Emily again? Was this the final chapter of my story with Brad?

Emily reached over and grabbed her bag and had one more thing left to say. "I didn't know what to expect coming here today. I did what Brad taught me to do: trust myself. I'm glad I did. Again, my gut has never been wrong. I can see why Brad felt the way he did about you. I am sure things didn't end the way either of you wanted them to, but I don't think the story is over just yet.

"I want you to know that after he stopped seeing you, he became very depressed. He submerged himself into his writing and he was on a mission to get so many things done before he could no longer function. The doctor gave him six months to live at the time of the diagnosis and he made it to ten months. I attribute that to you, Mackenzie, and for that I am truly grateful, and I thank you. He went downhill fast after August.

"At the end he told me he had accomplished everything on his bucket list except for one thing, and that would be up to Mackenzie. I don't know what that is, but I think it will be revealed in this gift he wanted me to give to you. I also have this to give you." She reached into her bag and pulled out a book. "What he was immersed in those last couple of months was another thing on his bucket list: writing a book. I think you'll find it very interesting. It is a collection of inspirational thoughts and quotes he'd collected throughout his whole life. He said he always had the intention of putting them into a book with the hope of inspiring others. He also told me that he put in a list of the wishes he'd made throughout the years when he saw shooting stars. He told me that when he looked over the list, he realized that they'd all been answered. The reason he hadn't realized it sooner was that they weren't always answered in the way he was expecting. But they were answered.

"In the front of the book, there is an envelope. In that envelope are two checks. One is part of some life insurance money I received. That is from me to you. The second check is from his book publisher. Through everything he was going through, he still got his book published. He told me that he wanted me to split the royalties from the book with you. After all, it was all of our stories and he wasn't going to need his share anyway."

Neither of us felt like laughing but we still couldn't help it. Emily went on to finish what she had to say. "He told me to give you a big hug from him and to tell you to go full speed ahead like a Mack truck." She gave me a hug, and after she pulled away, she came back and gave me another hug and said that one was from her. She smiled, paused, and then she walked out the door. Suddenly, I had never felt so alone.

Chapter 28

THERE WAS NOTHING I WAS GOING TO DO AT THE store that evening. I just wanted to go home and collapse into a coma. I had just completed what felt like an entire lifetime of intense conversation in one day. There was nothing left in my gas tank; I was completely spent. I went out to my pickup truck and drove home. I'm not sure how I got there because I don't remember anything about that drive. I hadn't eaten anything all day but when I got home, I was too tired to even think about fixing myself anything for dinner. I don't think I really cared anyway because I was still too busy running the day's conversation over and over in my head. What was in that last gift that Emily gave me that would complete Brad's bucket list? Could I somehow muster up enough energy to even go there tonight? Was I ready for that? Could I give it the full attention that it would need?

I decided I would put on my pajamas and get a good night's sleep and address the whole matter with a fresh mind the next day. However, before I even got my pajamas on, I knew there was no way I was going to be able to get any sleep until I finished this. I was still trying to debate this with myself, but my actions were preparing for the inevitable. I fixed myself a cup of hot chocolate with whipped cream and a cherry on top. It struck me that the last time I'd had a cup of hot chocolate like this was on Valentine's Day, when Brad brought it to me. Something inside of me was telling me that this was Brad's way of letting me know he wanted me to open his gift tonight.

Even after I had my hot chocolate and settled into my chair, I sat there staring at the package for probably fifteen minutes. I was afraid. I didn't think I had anything left in me, but my curiosity told me differently. I took a deep breath and took the package and ripped it open. It was a DVD. There was no label or writing on the case or the disc itself. I probably sat there another fifteen minutes just staring at the disc. I finally got up and put it into the player. It was probably another thirty minutes that I sat there with my finger on the play button before I took another deep breath and went for it. My heart was pounding and I couldn't breathe. I immediately pushed the stop button. It was probably another half an hour before I gathered up the courage to try again. That time I let it play.

It started with some rustling sounds in the background, but the picture frame was empty. It was about a minute before a person stepped into the picture. It had to be Brad, but it didn't look like him. Then I looked closer and I was sure it was him. He was very thin and pale. I was starting to cry when he put a cap on his head. I thought he was putting it on to cover up what was left of his head of hair, but it was more than that—it was the cap he wore to the store that had his name embroidered on it.

"I am wearing this cap in case you don't remember my name." It was just like him to lighten the mood and make me smile in any kind of situation. Brad was very nervous and fidgety; I guess I was, too.

He took a deep breath and finally started to talk. "There is a lot I wanted to say to you but I wasn't sure I would be able to get it all out so that is why I wrote the book for both you and Emily. I hope you will really see how I felt about you and that I never stopped feeling that way about you. I am so sorry for everything that happened to you. I hurt for you every single day. I wanted to be there with you more than you can ever know, but I couldn't. I know you don't hate me, but that wouldn't have mattered. It wouldn't have kept me away from you anyway. I knew you needed the space to get through all of it on your own. I also knew you could. I needed a reason to get out of your life. Not because I wanted to, but because I had to. You had lost your dad and you were going to be experiencing the worst time in your life. You didn't need to be living through my situation, too. I knew you were strong enough to handle it, but I wasn't strong enough to handle your pain. I didn't need you to worry about me. I was fine.

"Being with you had shown me a strength I never knew I had. Being with you brought me to my peace. And you know, when you have peace, everything in life, and death, is easier because life makes sense." There was a pause and he struggled to take a couple of labored breaths. This time it wasn't because of nerves; this time it was because he was weakening.

He looked back into the camera and said, "We better get on with this before I forget what I'm doing here. I don't know if you remember me telling you about how I used to lie out on my back porch as a young kid looking for shooting stars, but it was way back then that I started a bucket list. I didn't have any idea what that even was or that it was even a thing until a couple of years ago. Over the years, I kept adding to my bucket list and I was always looking for opportunities to accomplish things on the list and proudly scratch the achievement off. Whenever I saw a shooting star, I wished for something on my list. By going on my yearly vision quest, I felt like I was tracking my progress and my understanding of the things on my list. I was learning why things on my list were important to me and why I wanted to accomplish them. It was sort of a confirmation that I was on the right path in my journey. At the last vision quest when you were with me, I was able to scratch two of my biggest wishes off my list. The first, having you tell me how you admired me for having peace in my life. I didn't know that I had reached that place. You telling me made me recognize that accomplishment. The second thing: finding a soul mate. I had given up believing that soul mates even existed. I wasn't even sure what a soul mate was, but after being with you I had my answer. I knew what a soul mate was and I knew that it existed because of how I felt about you. That feeling never went away.

"There were only two things left on my bucket list after that: to write a book and perform a song on my own. I saved the hardest thing on my list for last, and for you. You never did tell me when your birthday is and with Christmas coming up, I decided I had to give you two things to make sure it was all covered. The first is the book. The book is two things: part journal of my time with you, and hopefully part inspirational guidebook. On many occasions you asked me what I had wished for and if they ever came true. As close as we were, the answers to those questions were very personal for me. For the most part, I never shared those experiences with anybody. That includes you and Emily. That is, until now.

"It doesn't really matter to me whether anybody believes my stories or lessons learned. But here is the truth I can share with you: they are all true and they work. Use them and make them work for you. Don't stop with just using the wisdom I discovered on my journey. Keep searching for and discovering new truths and wisdom for your own journey. Then do what I'm doing now: share that wisdom and wish with others so they can build off that foundation of truth for their own journey and then pass that on to others. My prayer here is for everyone to discover and experience the peace that I am now engulfed by. I know that is a highly improbable and unrealistic idealism, but I thought the same about soul mates. Never let go of hope. Every time you see a shooting star, make that wish. You don't see that many shooting stars, but they are still there. So, when you do see that shooting star, remember, my wishes came true, so make your wish. Then write your book and tell your story. Everybody has a story to tell.

"Now, the second thing, and the last thing on my bucket list." He walked out of the camera's view and I could hear him stumbling around until he came back holding a guitar. He was still trying to get situated and was clumsily banging the guitar into things. In traditional cute Brad style, he made me laugh. He took a couple of relaxing deep breaths and cleared his throat about a dozen times before he stopped and closed his eyes for a couple of seconds. Then, he opened his eyes and began to play.

It was an older song that I had heard before, but I wasn't really familiar with it. That didn't matter. It didn't matter who wrote the song or who sang it before or how well they performed it or how well Brad performed it. This one was for me. It was the most beautiful and exquisitely performed song I had ever heard or ever will hear. I will never forget it. It went like this:

Maybe I hang around here
A little more than I should
We both know I have somewhere else to go
But I got something to tell you
That I never thought I would
But I believe you really ought to know

I love you
I honestly love you

You don't have to answer
I see it in your eyes
Maybe it was better left unsaid
This is pure and simple
And you should realize
That it's coming from my heart and not my head

I love you
I honestly love you

I'm not trying to make you feel uncomfortable
I'm not trying to make you anything at all

But this feeling doesn't come along every day
And you shouldn't blow the chance to say
When you've got the chance to say

I love you
I honestly love you

If we both were born
In another place and time
This moment might be ending in a kiss
But there you are with yours
And here I am with mine
So, I guess we'll both be leaving it at this

I love you
I honestly love you
I honestly love you

When it was over, he paused for a few moments and then reached over to turn off the camera. Before he did, he took one last look straight into the camera. Without saying another word, he turned the camera off. That last lingering look is burned into my eternal memory.

I just sat there in total silence for a long time. It had been quite a day. I had lived a total lifetime in just one day. I couldn't tell you how I felt because I didn't know the answer to that. I had no idea how I should feel either. Was there even an emotion for that kind of thing? The amount of time this period of my life had taken was only a total of nineteen months. During four of those months there was no interaction between Brad and me. Such a short period of time and such a small number of days for such a long journey.

I thought for a moment about what lay ahead. Then, I smiled. The truth was that time was precious and I needed to stop worrying about the future and focus more on today. Tomorrow may never come but today was here and there was something I could do about that.

I took solace in the fact that Brad had left me his spirit in the book he wrote. The name of the book was *Shooting Stars: The Quest*. That was so appropriate on many different levels. I could take refuge in his wisdom that he'd recorded and passed on to me. I could trust that wisdom because I saw it. I could feel it. It was real. Then it hit me: not only did I see that truth and peace manifested through Brad, I realized that I had actually experienced it on a deeper level myself. The last night that Brad and I spent together at the vision quest, I saw a shooting star and made my wish. I asked him if he wanted to know what my wish was, and he said you couldn't tell anyone your wish until it came true. Well, I could now tell everyone my wish. It was to find true love.

I was still sitting in my chair, absorbed in so many thoughts and feelings, when I was interrupted by a ray of sunlight coming through the window. Was it morning already? I couldn't help but to start to smile. I was happy. I was at peace. I wasn't worried about my future. The sun was rising and it was a new day. Each day was precious, it was a gift. That day would always be a special gift. I had received the gifts of life, love, wisdom, peace, and happiness. That day also gave me an awakening to the power of giving. The irony of it: it was Christmas morning.

It was a day I would never forget. I would always celebrate this day for everything it represents on so many different levels. Brad was always trying to figure out my birthday and he never did while he was here on earth. Looking back, I wonder if he would have ever given me the kind of birthday surprise I gave him. Today, I found out. From wherever he was he gave me so many gifts for my birthday—more than I could ever imagine. Yes, today was also my birthday. I made one last wish, but it was a birthday wish. Brad always said that birthday wishes never came true, but since there was no shooting stars I could see, it was the best I could hope for. It was still the best birthday I'd ever had. Happy birthday to me!

THE END

Acknowledgements

BEING A FIRST-TIME AUTHOR THE LIST OF PEOPLE THAT should be recognized for their role in this project is beyond my scope of memory. I will start off by apologizing for all the names of people who I will forget to mention. To make sure I don't forget this first one-I will start with my wife Faith. Her role went way beyond the support and love from a devoted spouse. Without her subtle, and sometimes not so subtle, coaching and encouragement, this book would not have been done. For my birthday she signed me up for a four-week writing workshop, unbeknownst to me. Unbeknownst to her, the real gift was meeting author James Riordan.

James Riordan shared with me his expertise of many years as a successful author providing me with the critical editing and direction that contributed to the betterment of my story. He also gave me the courage and confidence to keep going. More importantly, I gained a new friend.

Then there is Janice Drew who is an old friend that I knew I could trust her judgement in an effort to determine if someone other than my wife liked the story. When her response was "that came out of Kevin's head?!", it gave me the extra incentive to move forward on this journey. Linda Phifer who placed a pre-order for three books (after she read the book), was another step to building my confidence to take a chance. There were a number of people that followed who gave me support, courage and strength to stay on course in many different ways-personally and professionally: Dan Abert, Donna Hecht, the Hess family, Lisa Miller, Jams Ballbach, Priscilla Lynch, Alyssa Nourie, Christina Loraine, Greg Thompson, and Mandy Madrox.

I certainly can't forget my friend Norm Sippel. Thank you for taking me on that Rocky Mountain high adventure to start it all.

I would like to thank Irving Music Inc., and Woolnough Music for granting me the permission to use the song lyrics.

I would also like to give a special mention to Caroline Macon Fleischer for going the extra mile with a publishing newbie. I look forward to working with her in the future.

From the beginning of this journey, the road was one of many personal obstacles that created detours all along the way. These detours made it clear what is truly important in life. If it weren't for all my friends, neighbors, and the doctors and nurses, I would have never reached this destination.

My family: my brother Richard (who paid me to list his name first), my sisters Cheryl and Linda. Our paths together and separately over the past five years have been extremely challenging and yet we have come through it all still speaking to each other. This includes my in-laws Lee, Carol and Guy Case who were inspirational in keeping this journey alive.

Finally, my mom and dad, Melvin and Mardell Spivey. They gave me life, they provided for me, they taught me, but most importantly they gave me no doubt that they loved me.

I thank God for all the people past, present and in the future, who have made and will make a difference in my life. May all of your wishes come true. Thank you.

About the Author

Kevin S. Spivey was born and raised in a small midwestern town an hour south of Chicago Illinois. After graduating from high school, he re-located to a number of different cities across the country before returning to his roots and settling down. He has spent most of his thirty-year professional career in human resources management before becoming an author. He calls himself an observer and student of life. As a writer it is his mission to turn those observations and lessons into interesting and entertaining stories that can inspire others to look at things from different perspectives. He seeks to challenge the reader to think at a deeper level and ask themselves harder questions to find more meaningful answers. In his role in human resources, he has conducted over a thousand interviews with prospective job applicants. Each of them with their own stories to tell and each one teaching him something. That education provides him with an infinite empirical history of experiences to provide material for thought provoking books to come.

For further information about the author and upcoming projects, visit his website at: www.kevinsspivey.com.